from willa,

with love

from the life of **WILLA HAVISHAM**

COLEEN MURTAGH PARATORE

SCHOLASTIC PRESS / NEW YORK

Library of Congress Cataloging-in-Publication Data

Paratore, Coleen, 1958–
  From Willa, with love : from the life of Willa Havisham / Coleen Murtagh Paratore. — 1st ed.
    p. cm.
  Summary: When her best friend Mariel and boyfriend JFK spend the summer away from Cape Cod, sophomore-to-be Willa, who works part-time in her family's inn, is unprepared for new romance and other surprises.
  [1. Dating (Social customs) — Fiction. 2. Summer — Fiction. 3. Hotels, motels, etc. — Fiction. 4. Cape Cod (Mass.) — Fiction.] I. Title.
  PZ7.P2137Fr 2011
  [Fic] — dc22

                                                            2010026573

ISBN 978-0-545-09405-4

10 9 8 7 6 5 4 3 2 1   11 12 13 14 15

Printed in the U.S.A.   23
First edition, July 2011

The text type was set in Sabon.
Book design by Lillie Howard

To everyone who has
loved a book and given
that gift to another.
From Cape Cod,
With Love,
☺ Coleen Murtagh Paratore

The books about Willa Havisham,
by Coleen Murtagh Paratore:

The Wedding Planner's Daughter
The Cupid Chronicles
Willa by Heart
Forget Me Not
Wish I Might
From Willa, With Love

Other books by the author that you also may enjoy:

Sunny Holiday
Sweet and Sunny
A Pearl Among Princes
The Funeral Director's Son
Kip Campbell's Gift
Mack McGinn's Big Win
26 Big Things Small Hands Do
Catching the Sun
How Prudence Proovit Proved the
Truth About Fairy Tales

Contents

CHAPTER 1

Nothing to Worry About

♥ ♥ ♥

A book is like a garden carried in the pocket.
— Chinese Proverb

I came across this quote: "A book is like a garden carried in the pocket," *and it made me think how a good book is a perennial thing; it lives on and on. Certain bits of the books we love sink into us like seeds in soil and mix with all the other seeds, and then who knows what colorful things might one day bloom.*

Recently I read a book called Three Cups of Tea *about a man who builds schools in remote mountain villages where children have no books, none. Loving books as much as I do, I cannot imagine a life without reading.*

More and more now as I watch the news or read the morning paper, I am drawn to stories about places in the world ravished by poverty or war or weather disasters, places where people have no food, no home, no books, and I think how fortunate I am to live in

1

this beautiful inn on Cape Cod with a happy family, delicious meals, a huge library, a warm snuggly bed with a stack of books on my nightstand, and I wonder, What can I do?

I stop writing, set down my pen, close my journal, *From the Life of Willa Havisham.* I glance at the clock. It's early yet. Maybe I can still catch the sunrise. There it is again. A walk by the water, the wind on my face, might send an answer . . . a direction. The sea is like a compass for me. It tells me where to go.

It's mouse quiet at the Bramblebriar Inn, which my mother, Stella Havisham, and stepfather, Sam Gracemore, manage here in the town of Bramble, on Cape Cod, Massachusetts. All of the rooms in the main building are full, as this is July, our busiest month. I walk softly down the hallway so I do not disturb our guests.

I smile as I pass the closed door of Room #7, the "Captain Ahab" room, where my newly discovered half brother, Will Havisham, is sleeping. Will is visiting here from England. Mother said he could be our guest for a while; I'm hoping a long, long while.

Will and I just met for the first time this summer when he came here to Cape Cod in search of our birthfather, Billy Havisham. Will believed our father was still alive and somewhere here on the Cape, and Will hoped that together we could find him.

It broke my heart to have to tell Will that our father was indeed dead, drowned in a hot-air balloon accident nearly fifteen years ago.

After being an only child my whole life, let me say, it was quite a shock to discover that I have a brother. Will is seventeen, three years older than me, but we share the same blue eyes, same brown hair, and, although we got off to a rocky start, he is proving himself to be quite a decent "chum," as Will would say.

It will be especially nice having Will around for the summer since my boyfriend, JFK — his name is Joseph Frances Kennelly and everyone calls him Joey, but I call him JFK in my head because he reminds me of President JFK, who loved Cape Cod — is in Florida staying with his grandparents for six weeks while he's doing some baseball internship his father arranged for him. My new best friend, Mariel Sanchez, is also off Cape for the summer, visiting her mother, who's starring in a Broadway show in Manhattan. I'm happy for Mare because she hasn't spent time with her mother in a long, long time, but still, that leaves me without my best friend.

Down the wide staircase, across the thick carpet, past the grandfather clock just now chiming five A.M.,

I smile at the sleeping golden polar bear blocking my exit out the front door. *Salty Dog.* My and Will's dog.

Salty followed me home from the beach earlier this summer. Mariel insisted he was a gift to me from the mermaids. She sees the world that way. When no one claimed Salty at the town shelter and after begging and begging my mother to let me adopt him, I discovered that Salty was Will's dog who had jumped ship when they anchored on Popponesset Beach. I was heartbroken having to give Salty up, but now that Will is staying here for a time, Salty can still be mine.

I kneel down and run my hand gently over his furry head, sniffing in his signature salty-seaweed smell. One big brown eye cocks open, then the other. He yawns, stands, shakes off doggy dreamland, and barks me a happy stinky-breath hello.

"Morning, Salty. Up for a walk? Let's go catch the sun."

I take my bike. Salty runs beside me.

In a few minutes we're at the shore.

"Ah, too late, we just missed it, Salty." I rest my bike against a rock and bend to breathe in the sweet cinnamon scent of the rugosa beach roses that grow wild all over the Cape. *Hmmm*, nice.

Standing at the top of the old gray beach stairs, I look out at the horizon.

The sun, a tiny orange ball of fire, is already too brilliant to look at.

Another new day has begun.

I close my eyes. *Thank you.*

What will this one bring?

Salty barks. I turn. There's someone back by the road, just now walking across the parking lot toward us and the beach.

"But we got here first, didn't we, Salty?"

He barks, *"Yep, that's right!"*

I laugh. "Good, come on, then. Let's make the first prints of the day."

CHAPTER 2

Something About Books

♥ ♥ ♥

Many a book is like a key to unknown chambers
within the castle of one's own self.
— Franz Kafka

If you want to catch the sun, you have to get to the shore early, before the sun rises out of the sea. Then, right at the very moment the sun first appears, when it's just a tiny diamond on the horizon, stare straight at it for a second and quickly close your eyes. At first there will just be white swirls in the darkness and then when they clear, you will see that tiny diamond in your mind. You caught the sun! Try it some time. It's amazing.

Salty and I were too late to catch the sun this morning, but the new dawn is still a wondrous thing to experience. I take a deep breath of good fresh air, looking up and down the beach, taking it all in, the sand, the sky, the water, the birds. . . . "So beautiful, Salty, huh?"

Salty barks, but he's distracted. He's trying to make friends with a seagull.

Just days ago I thought I might have seen a mermaid here in these waters. There was a young tourist girl who was adamant she had seen one. She drew quite a crowd of hopeful spectators and television crews even, she was so insistent, and I think my imagination began playing tricks on me.

Salty barks. The gull flaps its wings. Salty barks. The gull caws. Salty barks. The gull flies off. I laugh. "Sorry, buddy. Come on, let's walk."

I toss my sneakers by my bike and set off down the stairs. At the bottom there's a green pail and shovel left behind by a castle builder. There is also a book. I pick it up. The cover is wet from the tide. *James and the Giant Peach*, by Roald Dahl. Inside the cover, there's a girl's name printed neatly: RAYLEA JONES, 4B, SCHOOL 16, ATLANTA. Wow, that's far away. She must be visiting here; "4B" was probably her section of fourth grade. I wipe off the wet sand and set the book up on a high step to dry. Hopefully, Raylea will return for it. Or, if she's already back over the Bourne Bridge and gone home, perhaps another beachcomber will spot this treasure and happily start reading. How cool to find a book on the beach! I know I would have loved that in fourth grade, any grade actually.

Salty bounds along beside me, always ready for an adventure, and then he speeds off ahead. "Stay away from stinky stuff," I shout to him, knowing he'll do as he pleases.

Salty loves the sea so much, splash-running happily in and out of the water, he always smells like seaweed and fish, not exactly a pleasant perfume. Sometimes when Salty and I get back from our beach walks, my mother threatens to spray him with cologne or, worse, send him next door to the Sivlers' new poshy-posh pet spa, No Mutts About It, for a "top-to-tail makeover treatment." So far I have been able to spare Salty from that particular disgrace. Salty Dog is a sea dog, not a spa dog.

The water is placid this morning, just a soft *oooooofffff-wooshhhhh* as the waves roll in and out. The sand is cool beneath my bare feet. I spot a tiny piece of beach glass, a "mermaid tear" blue, my favorite, and stick it in my pocket for my rainbow jar at home. I collect beach glass: blue, white, green, and brown, and jingle shells, the orange ones (I think they are the prettiest). When the light streams through the glass jar on my window, it makes tiny rainbows all around my room.

A duck-plane makes a smooth landing on the water. Small black fish gallop after one another just offshore, flipping up and down in a school-straight line. Something splashes loudly back behind me and I turn to look.

Nothing.

Just last week I heard strange laughter, a light sing-songy giggling, saw something splash, felt an unexplained spray of water here and there . . . and wondered . . . could there be a mermaid? Was that tourist girl correct? Anything is possible, right? But no, I never saw a mermaid.

Too bad Mariel isn't here this summer. She would see the mermaid, for sure.

Salty bolts off way up the beach ahead of me, then stops, already finding a tasty treasure. He noses in and then he's eating. Salty Dog is the only dog I know who likes fish. I think Salty Dog was Salty Cat in a former life.

When I reach my dog, I see he's found some bloody fresh sushi for breakfast, which looks like a striped bass that met with a fishing hook or some larger fish with sharper teeth. I look at the fish's beautiful eye.

"No, Salty. Come on." I pull on his collar to drag him away. "We'll get breakfast at home."

I walk on, thinking about JFK so far away in Florida, wondering how his internship with that baseball team is going. I hope he's having a good time. I also hope that girl named Lorna who called to ask me what kind of cake to get JFK for his birthday last week has gone home to wherever girls named Lorna Doone live.

JFK said she was just the granddaughter of one of his grandparents' country club friends and they thought it would be nice for him to meet some kids his own age.

Nice? No. Not nice at all. Nice is dinner at your grandparents' club. Nice is a movie with your grandparents after. Nice is not a girl who gets you a cake for your birthday when you've only just met her and when you have a perfectly nice girlfriend back home on Cape Cod who is planning a surprise party for you when you return next month.

His grandparents meant no harm, JFK tried to reassure me. "You've got nothing to worry about, Willa."

Nothing to worry about. Are you kidding? This is me, Willa the worrier. I am the world's all-time undefeated worrying champ. I have won Olympic gold medals and Academy Awards and Heisman Trophies for my excellence in worrying. I have never been in a situation or met a person, place, or thing I couldn't find something to worry about. "It's an Irish thing," my nana, Violet Clancy, says. Nana runs Sweet Bramble Books, the book and candy shop on Main Street. An

Irish thing, maybe — I'm half English, too, and all-American — but worrying is most definitely a Willa thing.

I won't stop worrying until JFK is back home here in Bramble.

What kind of name is Lorna Doone anyway? Cookie girl.

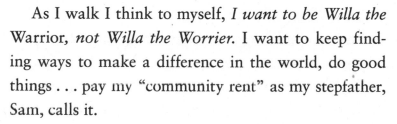

As I walk I think to myself, *I want to be Willa the Warrior, not Willa the Worrier.* I want to keep finding ways to make a difference in the world, do good things . . . pay my "community rent" as my stepfather, Sam, calls it.

And so back to my earlier journal question . . . *What can I do?*

I think of the book I just found on the beach. Something about books. That would make sense.

My friend Sulamina Mum (who was the minister at BUC, Bramble United Community, our nondenominational church here in town, before she got married and moved to South Carolina) would always say that when you are looking for a way to serve, find something that you really care about.

I really care about books.

I miss Mum. She was my first real friend when Mother and I moved here to Bramble. Mum's nephew Rob, a freshman at Boston College, is here on Cape for the summer. My friend, former best friend, Tina, and her new best friend, my nemesis, Ruby Sivler, whose family owns the pet spa, have major crushes on Rob and also on my brother, Will. Those girls are totally boy crazy. How can you like two boys at once?

I miss Mariel. We have a lot more in common, like walking on the beach and reading good books, for example.

The sun is moving up higher now. It casts a basket of diamonds across the blue waves. *"Here, Willa, catch!"* The diamonds come closer and closer until they reach my feet. I scoop them up in my hands. I'm a millionaire.

Now . . . What can I do?

It's only July. School doesn't start until September; I'll be a sophomore at Bramble Academy. JFK is away. Mariel is away. Tina and Ruby are totally focused on Rob and Will and the photography "book" they are making about the hottest lifeguards on Cape Cod. I only have to work four hours a day at the inn. That leaves lots and lots of free time. And so, *What can I do?*

There will be books and candy, of course, my two favorite things. Earlier this month, I set a goal of reading one book a day for the month of July — "skinny-punch books" I call them, books that only take a short time to read but pack a heavy punch that stays with you. Yesterday I reread Roald Dahl's *The BFG*, a favorite since fourth grade. I think briefly of Raylea Jones, the girl who left *James and the Giant Peach* on the beach. Has she read *The BFG*? I love how the giant collects dreams in jars.

When we reach the tip of the Spit, where the strong ocean current swirl-collides with the gentler bay, Salty and I turn and head back along the other side of this narrow strip of sandy land. Soon we come upon the little scallop-shaped spot where JFK and I had our first picnic. Closing my eyes, I smile, remembering how romantic it was. How we held hands and kissed.

There's chirping and a whoosh of wings, and a band of merry piping plover birds lands up ahead of me. As I near them, they swoop up and off again, afraid of me, the approaching giant. Silly little endangered birds.

I wish JFK were here. I touch the silver heart-shaped locket he gave me that Valentine's night in the barn. The night we first kissed and danced together. I open the locket, his face on the left, mine on the right. When I close it, we are kissing. I kick a rock. I miss him. Six whole weeks. More than half the summer, ruined. Stupid baseball.

I look up the beach, back toward the bluff where my bike is. There's someone standing there, too far away for me to tell if it's someone I know. And now where has Salty gone off to? Nowhere in sight. I climb up over the dune to the ocean side.

Sure enough, there's my dog, feasting on sushi again. When I call him he looks up, then lobs down and rolls around in the fish bones, giving himself a nice smelly sand bath for a lasting memory. On second thought, maybe Salty wasn't a cat in another life. Cats are always cleaning themselves. Salty seems to revel in smell.

I slap my thigh. "Come on, Salty. Let's go. Let's get you home for a bath."

My mother isn't a "dog person," as she says. I'm still amazed she let Salty stay. "Our guests don't want to smell *dog* when they enter the Bramblebriar Inn, Willa," she said. "Fresh flowers, yes, cookies baking, yes, lemon furniture polish, yes. . . . *Dog?* No!"

Almost as if Salty knows the trouble he'll cause me, he gallops into the water, swims out a bit, then turns and swims back in. He'll still smell like seaweed, but at least it won't be so fishy. "I'll race you, buddy!" I shout, and set off running. Salty sprints along beside me, spraying water all over my legs.

As we get closer to my bike, I look up at the person on the bluff. Is that Jess Farrelly? Tall, thin, long dark brown hair. He's in my class at Bramblebriar Academy. He has a band called the Buoy Boys.

Salty barks. I look down at him. Salty smiles. I swear that dog smiles.

When I look back up on the bluff, there's no one there. Was that Jess?

Salty barks, *"Me, me, pay attention to me."*

"I see you, buddy. I love you, Salty."

"You, too, you, too," he barks.

CHAPTER 3

Comings and Goings

♥ ♥ ♥

The great blessing of my youth was that I grew up in a
world of cheap and abundant books. There were books
in the study, books in the drawing room, books in the
cloakroom, books (two deep) in the great bookcase
on the landing, books in the bedroom, books piled high
as my shoulder. . . .
— C. S. Lewis

Rosie, our baker and Sam's assistant head chef, is in the kitchen when I get home.

"The cranberry-nut bread should be cool enough, Willa," she says, motioning to four loaves on racks on the counter. "Slice yourself a piece. I'll pour you a cup of tea."

"Thanks, Rosie," I say. "It smells delicious."

Rosalita Torres is an absolute genius baker of sweet things . . . pies, cakes, cookies, breads, muffins, cupcakes, puddings, soufflés. . . . I keep telling her she should have her own line of cookbooks and a television show. *Sweet Rosie Sweets* I tell her to call it. Mother gets annoyed when I praise Rosie so much because she doesn't want Rosie to leave us.

When Chickles Blazer, of the millionaire Buick Blazers, tasted the wedding cake Rosie made for her daughter Suzie-Jube's wedding here at the inn, Mrs. Blazer declared it was the best cake she'd ever tasted — and believe me, not to be rude or anything, Mrs. Blazer would attest to this herself, that lady has sampled many a cake in her life — and she said she was going to make Rosie "famous." This reminds me, I saw that Rosie got a letter from Mrs. Blazer recently. I spotted the return address when I brought in the mail.

"Hey, Rosie. I meant to ask you. I noticed you got a letter from the Blazers."

Rosie stops stirring whatever she's stirring. She looks out the window. "I've got one hundred desserts to make by that wedding Saturday," she says, starting to stir again. "The bride's a braviar, for sure."

"A braviar?" I say, spreading butter on the warm bread. "What's that?"

"You know, like they call some brides bridezillas because they are so monstrous, demanding this and that. Well, your mother said we should think of them as *braviars* — brides with caviar taste."

I roll my eyes. That's my mom.

"Stella likes braviars because they spend more," Rosie continues. "The Bennigan wedding this weekend, it's small, one hundred people, but wait until they get that bill. A six-course meal, lobster and filet mignon, top-shelf open bar, and one hundred individual — each one *unique* — tiny cakes for dessert. The bride insists that each guest receive a 'unique and completely original gourmet cake,' since each one of her guests is —"

"Wait, let me guess," I say. "Unique and completely original?"

"Yes." Rosie laughs and we both roll our eyes over that.

"Remember the cake you made for Suzie-Jube Blazer," I say, "the one that became our 'Signature Bramblebriar Wedding Cake'?"

Rosie smiles. "Yes, and you made it even more special putting those little silver lucky charms inside." Rosie locks eyes with mine. She bites her lip. She looks like she's going to cry.

"Rosie, what's wrong?"

She turns away. She turns back and looks at me.

Right then, I know. She's leaving us. I set down my teacup, wipe crumbs from my face. "Are we losing you?" I say.

Rosie tilts her head and smiles softly. "Yes, Willa. I'm sorry. I've thought about it long and hard. You know how much I love working here and how much you and Sam and, well . . . Stella . . . mean to me, but I have to think about my daughter, Lilly, and how best to provide for her and, well, the Blazers have made me an offer I simply cannot refuse."

"And what offer is that?" my mother says.

She and Sam have just entered the kitchen. My mother is standing there in her jogging clothes, hands on her hips, unsmiling, waiting for an answer. Sam pours two mugs of coffee, hands one to Mom, takes a sip of his, winks, and smiles *good morning* to me. I smile *good morning* back.

Rosie stands up. She paces around the kitchen as if to gain courage before speaking and then she stops and faces my mother. "The Blazers offered me a full scholarship to the college of my choice plus living expenses. I got accepted at the CIA, the Culinary Institute of America, in Hyde Park, New York, my first choice. . . ."

I think about how when the Blazers first visited the inn a few years back, I had just been named Community Service Leader for our class, and my friends and I were hosting a Halloween dance in the barn to help raise money to save the Bramble Library. The Blazers had such fun dancing (they came back again at Thanksgiving for more!) that they eventually donated a huge sum of money to the library, and then announced they were founding the Blazer Benevolent Foundation to offer college scholarships to deserving young people throughout the country. Now, that's what I call community rent.

Rosie is certainly "deserving." She's in her early twenties, a single mother, working full-time trying to support her little daughter, Lilly. . . . *And*, she has a very real and amazing gift for cooking. I know Rosie likes working here, but with a college degree and all that natural talent, who knows how far she can go?

"Oh, my gosh, Rosie, that's wonderful!" I leap up and rush over to hug her. Salty barks congratulations, too.

"Yes indeed," Sam says, stepping forward to shake Rosie's hand.

Rosie hugs Sam. She wipes a tear from her cheek. "I am so grateful, Sam, for all that you have done for me."

"I don't know what we'll do without our chief baker and assistant head chef," Sam says, "but we couldn't be more proud or happy for you, Rosie."

I love you, Sam. I smile at him.

My mother is silent. All eyes are on her.

I make a face at her like *Come on, Mom, say something.*

"When?" Mother says curtly to Rosie.

"I'd like to head up to Hyde Park this week, Stella, to start looking for an apartment and child care for Lilly."

"This weekend!" Mother shouts. "What about . . ."

"Stella," Sam says, cocking his head as if to say *Calm down, take a breath.*

"You can't possibly be thinking of quitting us here in the height of our busiest season, with the Bennigan wedding on Saturday and . . ."

"No, Stella," Rosie says. "I'll get the one hundred cakes done and I'll be back before the wedding and I'll stay on as long as I can, hopefully until you find a replacement."

"Do I have your word on that?" my mother demands. "That you won't just up and leave us stranded?"

"Mom," I say in a reprimanding tone. "We all want the best for Rosie."

My mother turns on me. "Yes, Willa, of course," she snaps, setting her mug down on the counter with a loud clank, "but I also want what's best for the Bramblebriar. I have a business to run here."

Salty makes a throaty-gurgling sound. Was that a growl?

My mother sniffs the air in Salty's direction. "And get that dog outside with a soap and a hose. He smells like dead fish."

"Sushi," I say under my breath.

Sam hears me. He laughs. "Come on," he says. "I'll help you."

"I'm off for my run," my mother says. "What about you, Willa? If you're going to run the Falmouth Road Race with me next month, you need to be training."

"I know," I say. "Maybe tomorrow." I don't feel like being my mother's running buddy right now. Not after she was so curt with Rosie. She should be happy for her!

After my mother leaves, Sam and Salty and I walk around the side of the inn to the backyard. Sam's circular garden Labyrinth is beautiful, flowers in full bloom, the tall white Shasta daisies, purple cone flowers, yellow Susans, and red roses all trying to beat out the striking blue hyacinths for "best of show," but the hyacinths take the blue ribbon today.

"I'll sure miss Rosie," I say to Sam as he unravels the long green garden hose.

"Me, too," Sam says. "I'll miss her friendship and her talent. We made a good team in the kitchen." He hands me the nozzle. He squeezes some soap onto Salty and reaches for a brush.

"Joey is gone, Mariel's gone . . . now Rosie, too. I'm excited for her, but how depressing. . . ."

Sam touches my arm to get my attention. "That's life, Willa," he says to me. "People we love, coming and going."

"I know, but . . ."

"Listen," Sam says. "I wanted to surprise you with the news early Sunday morning before church, but I think maybe you could use the good news right now."

"What news?" I say, turning on the nozzle.

"Sulamina Mum's coming back."

"What! Oh, my gosh, Sam, really?" I've got goose bumps. "When?"

"Sunday," Sam says. "The board made her a wonderful offer and she's coming back home to us."

"Whoopee!" I shout, aiming the stream of water straight up in the air and shaking it all around over our heads so it rains on me and Sam and our fishy-smelling sushi-loving dog.

CHAPTER 4

Stella Steps It Up

In books I have traveled, not only to other worlds, but into my own. I learned who I was and who I wanted to be, what I might aspire to, and what I might dare to dream about my world and myself.
— Anna Quindlen

Showering up and changing after the hose storm, still smiling ear to ear — Mum's coming back! Mum's coming back! — I report to the kitchen for breakfast duty.

After washing my hands, I put on a green Bramblebriar apron and review the main course specials Rosie has posted for the day:

*Bacon and Cheddar Omelet
with Cinnamon Swirl Raisin Toast
Blueberry-Strawberry Belgian Waffles
with Country Sausage
Spinach, Feta, and Tomato Quiche
with Fresh Fruit Cup*

Yum!

In addition to the main breakfast entrees, our guests may also help themselves from a long table filled with lighter fare: fresh granola, yogurts, assorted cereals, muffins, bagels, and fruit.

No one goes hungry at the Bramblebriar Inn.

I take a tray of cloth napkin–covered baskets filled with warm cranberry bread slices and small plates with pats of butter and I head to my post on the porch.

It's warm and sunny, with a robin-egg blue sky, a postcard-perfect summer day. Our guests will be so pleased. No one wants rain on vacation.

My four-hour shift will fly by in a flash and soon I'll be off to the beach with my lunch and today's skinny-punch book: *Hope Was Here*. It's by one of my favorite authors, Joan Bauer, about a girl named Hope who is a waitress. Given our similar professions, I thought maybe Hope and I could relate.

As each group of our guests wanders onto the sun-porch and chooses a table, I welcome them, set down the cranberry bread and butter, and fill their glasses with water. Directing them toward the specials on the chalkboard, I ask what kind of juice I can bring and would they like tea or coffee. When I return with their drinks, I take their main course orders, making friendly small talk, inquiring about what they did last night or what they have planned for today.

"Morning, little sister," Will says to me at the side service table, swiping two pieces of cranberry bread and chugging down a glass of orange juice I had just poured for the nice lady from Essex, Vermont.

"Hey, stop that," I say.

"See ya later," Will says.

"Where are you going?" I ask.

"Out to the Vineyard. Chauncey and I are going deep-sea fishing with his uncle."

Chauncey Southends is a friend of Will's from Bainbridge, the boarding school they both attend in England. Chauncey is visiting family on the island of Martha's Vineyard, a short boat or ferry ride from the Cape.

Will takes another juice from my tray.

"Hey!" I scold.

He laughs. "Don't work too hard, Willa."

"Don't fall off the boat!" I shout after him.

The white-haired lady from Albany, New York, a retired teacher, Mrs. Noonan, smiles and winks at me. "You tell him, honey," she says.

"What are your plans today, Mrs. Noonan?" I ask, refilling her cup of decaf coffee and checking to be sure there's still cream left in the pitcher. Remembering whether a guest drinks regular or decaf is an important part of this job.

"A walk in the Labyrinth, Willa," she says, "then a chaise in the shade by the pond with a book or two, maybe even three of them."

"Sounds perfect to me," I say.

The handsome, stylishly dressed young couple from New York City — she's an editor, he works in finance — ask me what's going on around town this week.

"The Barnstable Fair opens in East Falmouth," I say. "That's fun." I think how I won't be going with JFK, won't be riding the Ferris wheel at night, holding hands and . . .

Guests always ask me for suggestions of things to do on their vacation, and I am happy to recommend. I tell them about my favorite Cape beaches, South Cape and Old Silver here on the upper Cape; Nauset, Marconi, and Lifeguard on the outer Cape. I direct them to the most fun mini-golf places, the best lighthouses, favorite biking routes along the Cape Cod Canal or on the Rail Trail or the Shining Sea Bike Path from Falmouth to Woods Hole, or possibly a walk on the nature trails here on conservation lands or out through the National Seashore. And then there's always a ferry ride to Nantucket or Martha's Vineyard, a seal watch out of Chatham, a whale watch from Provincetown, and a visit to Pilgrim Monument.

If it's a rainy day, I send guests first stop to Sweet Bramble Books, where often Nana will be hosting a visiting author for a signing, or to one of the other bookstores up and down the Cape, which always host events. Or, for those who like to shop, I point them toward nearby Mashpee Commons or to the towns with quaint main streets filled with great shops and restaurants, and then there are all of the art and antique galleries, and the museums, my favorite being the Kennedy museum in Hyannis, given my love for all things "JFK." And they absolutely must try candlepin bowling and take a tour of Cape Cod Potato Chips, where they give each visitor a free bag of chips; the movie theaters; the mall; and, of course, our very own Bramblebriar Inn Library stacked floor to rafters with books, managed by yours truly; and our game room, also managed by yours truly, stocked with every board game you can imagine, my favorites being Scrabble, chess, and Chinese checkers.

When the last party has finished breakfast and the tables are cleared and dishes all stacked in the dishwashers, I head up to my room to change for the beach. The door to my parents' bedroom is open. As I approach, I hear them talking.

"We're down, Sam," Mother says. "We've got serious money troubles. Occupancy's off. The main house is full, but four of the other buildings are empty. Dinners are down ten percent. The weddings have gotten too folksy-homey."

Folksy-homey? I pause to listen.

"I'm getting back into high-end weddings," my mother says. "I once was the crème de la crème . . . a wedding planner with a mile-long waiting list. We should be getting two hundred dollars a head for meals alone, before the music and entertainment and . . ."

Two hundred dollars a person? So, for a wedding with two hundred guests, that would be $40,000 for dinner alone? No wonder Sulamina Mum and Riley said they couldn't afford to have their wedding here. No wonder Sam's sister, Ruthie, and her fiancé, Spruce, requested such a modest affair. Wow, the Blazer wedding must have cost a fortune! They had more than three hundred guests, as I recall.

"The charms in the cake thing is sweet," my mother is saying, "but it's not bringing in top-shelf clientele. Wealthy clients want fresh and original. They want to be pampered. They want to know their wedding is a singular work of art."

What? That's insulting. Those charms were my idea. The wedding magazines said it was "adorable."

"I'm going to start stepping it up here, Sam," my mother says. "The economy's down, tourism's off, but a wedding is a wedding, and that's where the money is. Nobody wants to disappoint a bride. We haven't had a caviar wedding since Suzie Blazer. . . ."

My heart is pounding. There she goes again. My mother the business barracuda. I wonder how long it will be before she gets restless with the slower, simpler life here at the inn. Mother was born and raised on the Cape, but when she left for college, she was planning on leaving for good. Nana said my mother thought the Cape was too quaint and old-fashioned, and that wasn't a good thing. Stella wanted a more exciting, fast-paced, big-city cosmopolitan life. After my birthfather, Billy Havisham, died, she started Weddings by Havisham and quickly became one of the most successful wedding planners in the country. But her heart was so broken by Billy's death that she swore off ever loving, ever marrying again. Each time she got close to a new suitor, she'd freak out and close up shop and move us to another city. Finally, Nana urged Mom to come on home, and we moved here to Cape Cod. Lucky for me, my eighth-grade teacher, Sam Gracemore, turned out to be just the perfect match for my mother. They say opposites attract. Sam and Stella are proof of that. And I was the one who set them up on their first date.

Oh, no. . . . What if my mother wants to leave Cape Cod and move us to a big city again? What about our inn? What about the plans Sam told me he and Mom have to possibly adopt a baby? What if I have to leave JFK and Mariel and . . .

Reason: Stop it, Willa.

Willa: But —

Reason: You're getting ahead of yourself.

Willa: But —

Reason: No more worrying. Be a *warrior.*

Willa: But —

Reason: You were headed to the beach with *Hope.* Now go.

Willa: Oh, *all right.*

CHAPTER 5

Not a Date or Anything

♥   ♥   ♥

I wrote my first novel because I wanted to read it.
— Toni Morrison

Having hit Poppy Beach this morning, this afternoon I head for South Cape.

The beach is packed. I have to walk out quite a ways until I find a quiet spot apart from little kids playing ball or music blaring.

I spread my towel and sit down to eat my lunch — a turkey sandwich, dill pickle, blueberries, Cape Cod potato chips, and one of Rosie's chocolate-toffee-chunk cookies. I think about Rosie, how much I'm going to miss her, but how happy I am for her and Lilly.

Slathering up with sunblock, I lie on my stomach, book propped, and read until I get sleepy. I roll over on my back to take a nap.

Later I feel something tickling my face and when I open my eyes, Tina and Ruby are standing over me. Ruby has a seagull feather in her hand. I push the feather away, wipe drool from my mouth, and sit up.

Ugh, don't you hate it when you realize someone's been watching you sleep?

They have also buried my legs in sand. I guess they thought that was funny, too. They stare at me, giggling.

"Where's your brother?" Ruby asks, adjusting her earrings.

"Fishing," I say, brushing the sand off my legs.

"I wish he'd catch me," Ruby says, tossing back her mermaid-long red hair.

"No, me," Tina, says, laughing, tossing back her mermaid-long blond hair.

"He hasn't hooked up with anyone here yet, has he?" Ruby says.

"She means, is he dating anyone?" Tina clarifies as if I am in kindergarten.

"Will just got here," I say, and then I can't resist. "Besides, he's dating the daughter of a duke back in England."

"Really?" Tina and Ruby say, eyes popping, mouths dropping in awe, my hunky half brother's star soaring even higher in their hot-boys universe.

No, just a little white lie, which never hurt a sand fly, as Nana says.

"What's her name?" Tina says.

"I don't know," I answer.

"And what about black beauty?" Ruby says. "Where's he?"

"Who?" I ask, my head still fuzzy from the nap, surprised at Ruby making any sort of literary reference. My nose feels burned; I reach up to touch it.

"That gorgeous black college guy you were talking to the other day," Ruby says. "We heard you inviting him to your house for dinner."

She's talking about Sulamina Mum's nephew, Rob. I invited him to Bramblebriar knowing Sam and Mom would love to meet him since he was related to Mum. *Black beauty.* Rob would smile about that. Ruby's right; he is beautiful, tall, muscular, with tightly cropped hair, tiny diamond stud earrings, a gold cross on a chain around his neck. *Black beauty.* Leave it to Ruby.

"How would I know where he is?" I say.

"It's important that we find him, Willa," Tina says, hands on her hips, tossing her blond mane back again for emphasis.

"That's right," Ruby says, hands on hips, tossing her hair back, too. "We need to interview him for our book."

I stifle a laugh at the word *book* for Tina's sake only. Tina Belle was my best friend all that time before she and Ruby found more in common and I found

Mariel. Their "book" is nothing more than a cheesy album sort of thing with photos of cute boys posing on lifeguard thrones or picking up a raft or running in or out of the waves. The captions underneath describe some of their favorite things, foods, cars, bands, and their favorite places to take girls on dates. Tina and Ruby are sure their "book" will be a bestseller. They want me to get Nana to sell it in her store.

"He's stationed here at this beach, right?" Ruby says.

Rob is such a nice guy. He's already complained about Tina and Ruby annoying him. He doesn't want to be in their silly book. I have half a mind to send Ruby on a wild goose chase, to tell her "no, he's stationed out at Coast Guard beach," way out on the outer Cape, but that wouldn't be very nice. And I've already told them one big fat whopping fib about Will and the duke's daughter.

"Yes, I think Rob works here at South Cape," I say. "Maybe he has the day off."

Ruby raises her sunglasses and squints at me like she's trying to determine if I'm telling the truth. "Are you sure you don't know where he is?"

"Scout's honor, Ruby," I say.

Ruby rolls her eyes at me and readjusts her shades.

"And when will Will be back from fishing?" Tina says.

"I don't know," I say, shrugging my shoulders. "I guess when he catches something."

Tina sighs. Ruby sighs. No boys here. Their work is done.

Then Ruby feels the spark of an idea. "Come on, Teen, there's my dad's boat. I'll get him to ride us over to the Vineyard. Maybe we can find Will."

And they're off.

I send a warning to my brother across the waves. *Hide, Will, hide.*

"See ya later, Willa." Tina throws a bone back to me as she and Ruby walk away.

"Yeah. See ya later."

I read some more *Hope*, then touch up my sunblock and head up the beach for a walk. Salty must have gone out on the fishing boat with Will. The Southends better have a heavy lid on the ice chest where they put their catch or Salty'll be having sushi for lunch today, too. I bend to pick up a green mermaid tear and when I stand back up I see a boy walking toward me.

It's Jess Farrelly; this time, I'm sure it's him. His and Luke LeGraw's band, the Buoy Boys, used to stink, but they're really good now. Jess is the drummer.

"Hey, Willa, what's up," he says, stopping to talk.

"Nothing much," I say, noting how cute he is, his dark hair long and windblown, a leather rope choker around his neck, cutoff jean shorts with holes ripped in them. He looks like a model for Abercrombie & Fitch. He even smells good.

Jess is staring at me. He isn't one to make idle chatter. In fact, he rarely ever talks. The girls at school think he's mysterious, sexy.

"Were you by any chance at Popponesset Beach this morning?" I say.

"Yeah, that was me," he says. "I saw you."

The way he says this makes my stomach flutter.

"You and Joe still tight?" Jess says, his brown eyes deep and brooding like I suppose a drummer's should be.

My stomach flips. "Yes."

"I heard he's in Florida all summer," Jess says.

I gulp and glance away from those eyes. "He'll be back soon," I say.

Why am I so nervous?

Jess picks up a shell and throws it into the water.

I notice the muscles on his tanned arm.

"Luke and I are playing over at Poppy Marketplace in New Seabury Friday night. Want to come?"

My heart beats faster. *He's asking me on a date?*

"Not a date or anything," Jess says as if reading my mind. "It'll be just a bunch of tourist kids dancing; you know the crowd there. It's a benefit for —"

"No," I say, cutting him off. "I can't." That sure sounds like a date to me.

"Got other plans?" Jess asks.

Those brown eyes are absolutely mesmerizing. I've known this boy for years now; why haven't I noticed how cute he is? Maybe he is just asking as a friend. . . . And then I think of JFK. *My boyfriend, JFK.* He'll be calling later today. No, Willa, say *no*.

"No!" I shout. "I mean, *yes*."

Jess looks puzzled. "What?"

"Yes, I have other plans. Sorry."

"No worries," he says, his brown eyes holding my blue ones in a lock. He searches my face as if he's trying to determine something. He shrugs his shoulders, clears his throat, and spits. "Some other time maybe. See ya around." And off up the beach he walks.

"Yeah, sure. See you around."

I watch him walk away.

I wanted to say yes.

Later, back at the inn, I change into my running gear and do three miles. I keep picturing Jess's face. Why? *Stop it, Willa. Cut it out.*

When I get back from my run, there's a lady, a man, and three kids, tourists most likely, standing in front of our Bramble Board. This is the display board we have on the lawn out in front of the inn. Sam started it, but now it's my job to change the inspirational messages. Today it reads:

> *If there is to be peace in the world*
> *There must be peace in the nations.*
> *If there is to be peace in the nations*
> *There must be peace in the cities.*
> *If there is to be peace in the cities*
> *There must be peace between neighbors.*
> *If there is to be peace between neighbors*
> *There must be peace in the home.*
> *If there is to be peace in the home*
> *There must be peace in the heart.*
> — Lao Tzu, 570–490 B.C.

At night when JFK calls, I start to tell him about running into Jess Farrelly on the beach, but then I don't.

I lie awake a long time, feeling something other than peace in my heart.

CHAPTER 6

The Hot-Pink Sneakers

♥　♥　♥

When you sell a man a book, you don't sell him twelve ounces of paper and ink and glue — you sell him a whole new life. Love and friendship and humor and ships at sea by night — there's all heaven and earth in a book, a real book I mean.
— Christopher Morley

When I wake the next morning, I look around my bedroom, my eyes resting on the jug with the yellow top on which I've written CHANGE FOR GOOD ✪.

I bought the jar — it was labeled for making sun tea — at the dollar store, then cut a hole in the top. I dumped in all of the coins from my dresser drawers, purses, and school backpack, emptied out my jeans and coat pockets. I'm going to keep putting all of my spare change in there until it's full and then I'm going to give the money to a good cause and start filling the jug all over again.

I was inspired to make CHANGE FOR GOOD ✪ after

reading that book, *Three Cups of Tea*. Funny, isn't it, how a book can affect you like that?

I made CHANGE FOR GOOD ✪ jugs for Sam and Mom and Nana, and then several staff members here at the inn asked for them and then my teacher, Dr. Swaminathan, and . . . the idea sort of took off, especially when Sam shared the idea at BUC, where he has been filling in as guest minister while the board looks for a replacement for Mum.

Mum! Oh, my gosh. I can't wait to hug her! And Riley, her husband, such a great guy.

I think about what I was writing yesterday morning in my journal, about how I want to find my next way to make a difference in the world. *What can I do?* And then I got sidetracked with Rosie going and Mum coming and Tina and Ruby crushing on Will and Rob . . . and then with Jess on the beach. Was he asking me on a date? He said no, but it sure felt that way.

But what am I going to do? What's my next community rent? I better come up with something soon. Mum will certainly ask me on Sunday.

Something involving books. That I know. I look at my bookcase, stocked floor to ceiling with all of the books I've read and loved. They are like friends to me, truly.

I get up and go look out the window. Overcast and cloudy, it won't be a beach day, good thing. I got too much sun yesterday. My nose will be peeling for sure.

After breakfast duty, I bike into the center of town.

Bramble was once a thriving seaport village, home of the famous whaler Mitticus Bramble. There are many original homes standing, mostly brick, and some of the side streets are still cobblestone.

Tall, white-columned Bramble United Community borders one end of Main Street. BUC used to be a congregational church, but now it is nondenominational, welcoming people of all backgrounds and beliefs.

The old ivy-covered stone Bramble Free Library, with its reading garden and whale spoutin' fountain, stands guard on the opposite end of Main Street.

I wonder what my librarian friend Mrs. Saperstone is reading this week? She has been dating my English teacher from Bramble Academy, Dr. Swaminathan. I just love "Dr. Swammy," as I call him. I sort of had a hand in matching them up and I've been coaching Dr. Swammy a bit on what sort of candy he should buy for Mrs. Saperstone and that yes, indeed, he should show up at the library programs she plans. *Geesh*, that man is Rhodes-Scholar book-smart, but, boy, is he rusty in the romance genre.

Dr. Swammy is helping Nana part-time in her store

for the summer. Good thing, because my gramp, who died recently, managed the book part of Sweet Bramble Books; Nana runs the "sweets" side. Dr. Swammy has become a huge help to Nana, ordering and recommending books and signing up authors for events. Jane Yolen's coming this summer.

I just love my town. In between BUC and the library, lining Main Street on both sides are various stores, restaurants, and clothing shops; Bloomin' Jean's ice cream; Hairs to You hair salon; two art galleries; Wickstrom's jewelry store, where JFK bought my locket; Fancy's fish market, where Salty would love to work; Cohen's card shop; the pharmacy; a movie theater; a few tourist shops; and the hands-down best store on all of Cape Cod: Sweet Bramble Books.

As I pass by Lammers' clothing store, something in the window catches my eye. Sneakers. Hot-pink sneakers. I stop and stare at them.

Oh, my gosh, I love them. They are calling to me. *"Willa, come buy us, hurry!"*

Now, as my friends and my mother will be the first to attest, I hate to shop for clothes. It's a painful experience for me. I never think I look good in anything. I can never decide what style or color. But those pink sneakers? They are mine. I can see myself in them. It's as if they're already on my feet.

I go in the store. They have my size. I try them on and test-walk about. I feel wonderful. The clerk puts my old sneakers in the box, and I wear my pink back out onto Main Street. And just as I do, the sun comes out and I can hear bluebirds tweeting and angels singing. Just kidding. But this is a very nice new feeling.

Maybe my dreadful shopping days are done? Maybe this is the start of a whole new Willa?

Yellow is my current favorite color; maybe I'm moving on to pink.

CHAPTER 7

The Good Ones

♥ ♥ ♥

I was born with the impression that what happened in books was much more reasonable, and interesting, and real, in some ways, than what happened in life.
— Anne Tyler

When I enter Nana's store, her scruffy black-and-white dog, Scamp, slip-bounds over the hardwood floor to greet me. I kneel down so he can lick my face. I laugh. "Hey, Scamp, hey, buddy."

Scamp lies on his back, four paws in the air, and I rub his stomach the way he likes. I see his sister, Muffles, the old, gray fluffy cat who is always sleeping, over there in her usual spot in the window, basking in the sun, purr-snoring.

"Willa!" Nana calls over to me. "Come give me a hug, shmug."

A customer hears Nana and smiles.

"Nice sneakers," Nana says to me.

"Thanks."

"Did you hear the good news?" Nana asks as she slides a fresh tray of dark chocolate–covered apricots into the glass display case.

Nana is on the board at BUC; she must be talking about Mum coming back.

"Yes," I say. "I can't wait to see her!"

"Her?" Nana says. "You mean him. Last time I checked, James Taylor was a him."

"*James Taylor?*" I say. "The singer?"

"Yes." Nana laughs. "He has a new book out and Dr. Swaminathan booked him for a signing Saturday. Mr. Taylor has a brother out on the Vineyard and he'll be doing a tour of some Cape stores. But we got him first. Isn't that grand?"

"Awesome, Nana. Way to go!"

"And you heard Mum's coming back," Nana says, weighing out a customer's order of penuche fudge and placing it into a white-and-gold-lettered Sweet Bramble Books box, tying it up with a gold bow.

"Yes," I say. "I can't wait to see her! We should have a party for her."

A customer asks Nana for a special assortment of her famous saltwater taffy, which he read about in *Cape Cod Life* magazine, for a housewarming gift.

"This is my granddaughter, Willa," Nana says. "It was her idea to tie little happy messages on our taffies like Hershey's Kisses tags. That's how we finally won the Best Sweets on the Upper Cape Award. Next, we're aiming for Best Bookstore. . . . Falmouth, Brewster, and Sandwich keep inching us out, but we've got an all-star cast of authors appearing here this month . . . Meg Cabot, Mary Higgins Clark, Laurie Halse Anderson, Jerry Spinelli. . . ."

The man shakes my hand. "I'm Stanley Hadsell. Nice to meet you. I manage a bookstore in Troy, New York. Market Block Books."

"Another indie, huh?" Nana says, referring to independent bookstores. "Good. We should compare notes, Stan."

♥   ♥   ♥

I head over to the book side of Sweet Bramble to find Dr. Swammy.

There are three or four customers milling about. Dr. Swammy is standing behind the register. He smiles as he writes something inside the front cover of a red-jacketed book. He looks up and sees me. He closes the book quickly and slides it under the counter, which of course makes me curious to know just what he's reading.

"Hi, Dr. Swammy."

"Hello, Willa. Good to see you. I've got some book suggestions for you."

"Great, thanks," I say.

Dr. Swammy reaches to the shelf behind him, finds the stack he's looking for, peels off the yellow sticky note that says *Willa*, and hands me some books.

When Gramp Tweed was alive, he was the one I counted on to bring "the good ones," as he called them, to my attention. I'd come here every Friday after school and we'd sit on that couch over there and drink lemon tea, no milk or sugar, and "book-talk" about the characters and themes, and what we liked or didn't. Now Dr. Swammy and Mrs. Saperstone are my reading coaches. Between the two of them, I know I'll never be without a good book to read, and that's a very comforting thought. No matter what changes, or who comes and goes in my life, I will always have my books.

I check out the covers: *Out of the Dust* by Karen Hesse; *Ella Enchanted* by Gail Carson Levine; *Kira-Kira* by Cynthia Kadohata; and *Everything on a Waffle* by Polly Horvath. I notice they all have a gold or silver Newbery medallion on the cover; these are the highest honors awarded to authors of books for young readers.

"Thanks, Dr.," I say. "What do I owe you?"

"Now, you know better than that, Willa. Your grandmother would never hear of it. She is delighted you are such a voracious reader, and as you know, I am as well. I predict we'll be stocking books written by you in this very store one day."

"Do you really think so, Dr. Swammy?"

I remember my gramp used to always tell me that. He said to read the best books while I was young and then one day I would write some. He gave me my first journal and I've been writing ever since, chronicling the best and worst from the life of Willa Havisham.

Soon after my beloved gramp died, I saw this startling red cardinal. We had a connection, me and that bird. Now, whenever I spot a cardinal, I think of Gramp up in heaven, watching over me, making sure God reads "the good ones."

"You might want to think about putting book plates in the books in your collection," Dr. Swammy says, handing me a packet of square stick-on labels that read FROM THE LIBRARY OF: . . . "Then, when you loan your books out, they'll be sure to make their way back to you."

"But I don't like to loan my books," I say, not that any of my friends ever ask to borrow them, except occasionally Mariel.

"Really?" Dr. Swammy says. "That's surprising. Why?"

"My books are my most important possessions. I

write in them as I'm reading them — scribbled notes in the margins, smiley faces, 'me, too's! Someday, I'll look back and remember how I was feeling then, what I was thinking then. . . ."

"Excuse me," says a customer behind me. She's looking at Dr. Swaminathan. "My nine-year-old grandson is coming to visit this week. I know he says he likes series, but I can't remember the names. Can you recommend some books?"

"Certainly," Dr. Swammy says. "Right this way."

He leads the lady to the middle-grade series section. "The Chet Gecko books are popular with that age group," Dr. Swammy says, "and the Hank Zipzer books are funny. If he's into sports, he'll like the Matt Christopher books, or if he's into fantasy, he might enjoy the Percy Jackson. . . ." And then they are out of earshot, and I rush to sneak a peek at that red book Dr. Swammy was writing in.

It's a book of love poems. I open the cover.

My Dearest Leslie,
　There are no words to express my love for you.
　Only poetry approaches.
　Please say you will do me the honor of taking my hand in

And then it's cut off. Dr. Swammy stopped writing when he saw me. Oh, my gosh, how sweet! The last word was obviously going to be *marriage*. *Please say you will do me the honor of taking my hand in marriage.* He's finally going to ask Mrs. Saperstone to marry him! Oh, how wonderful. Two of my favorite people tying the knot. Oh, they must have their ceremony at BUC. It will be the first wedding Mum will officiate upon her return. And they absolutely must have their reception at the Bramblebriar. I will plan it, of course, out by the Labyrinth, under white tents, with twinkle lights strung from the trees and —

"*Willa,*" Dr. Swaminathan says, returning to the counter. His eyes rest on the book in my hand. His face reddens. He adjusts his turban. He coughs.

"I'm sorry," I say, mortified. I had no right to invade his privacy. I close the red book and put it back under the counter. "Please forgive me, Dr. Swammy. My curiosity got the better of me."

"You are forgiven," he says in his quiet, distinguished voice. "May I please ask you, though, to keep this matter . . ."

"Oh, absolutely, Dr. Swammy. Your secret is safe with me. I wouldn't want to spoil the surprise. Oh, no. I would never do that!"

"I like your sneakers," says the lady Dr. Swammy

was helping. "That color pink with the white laces." She's holding several books. Dr. Swammy did a good job. Some nine-year-old boy is going to be so lucky when his family crosses that roller-coaster Bourne Bridge to his grandmother's house and he finds a stack of great books waiting for him.

Dr. Swammy looks down at my new pink sneaks. "Yes, they are quite striking," he says. "Colorful."

"Thanks for the books, Dr. Swammy. And the labels. I won't use them for my personal collection, but I'll put them in the books in our inn library. Thank you."

I pop back over to the candy side of the store to get a bag of saltwater taffy, thinking how I'll lie on my bed on this cloudy afternoon and read and chew until dinnertime. I wanted to stop in and see Mrs. Saperstone at the library, but I can't risk my face giving the surprise away. They say you can't judge a book by its cover, but you can always judge me by my face. I find it impossible to mask my feelings.

I am so excited for them! Wedding bells are in the air!

Riding back home I nearly collide a few times looking down at my new pink sneakers. My beautiful new hot-pink sneakers.

CHAPTER 8

Will's Wild Goose Chase

♥ ♥ ♥

*There is nothing on earth more exquisite than a bonny
book, with well-placed columns of rich black writing in
beautiful borders, and illuminated pictures cunningly
inset.*

— George Bernard Shaw

Salty Dog looks up from his nap when I bound up
the front porch steps to the inn. Right away I know
something is wrong. Walking over to pet him, I see he's
wearing a bright green bow around his neck, his golden
fur looks newly brushed and shinier, and lo and behold,
he doesn't smell like fish.

"Oh, no, she didn't, did she, Salty?"

My mother took him to the Sivlers' spa, No Mutts
About It.

Salty looks at me and puts his head down, ashamed.
I put my arms around his thick neck and hug him.
He smells like fancy soap or spices or something. He
doesn't smell like Salty Dog. He doesn't smile at me.

"Was it really awful?" I ask him, thinking about all of those foo-fooey silly hot dog–size dogs I see coming in and out of that place, their owners cooing over them. I look over at the spa where just now, Mrs. Sivler is walking out the front door. She's holding her looks-like-a-toy white poodle, Pookie. She's wearing a short-short red sundress, scooped low in the front, way too young a look for a lady her age, and she has tied a matching red bow around Pookie's neck. *Puke, puke.*

Salty makes a whimpy-whiny sound, probably remembering the horrors.

"Did they make you feel like you were a mutt because you'd never been to a spa before?" I say, untying the green bow from Salty's neck. At least they thought to give him a green bow, green and gold being our signature colors here at the inn. "Did they give you a massage and plunk you in a bubble bath and make you eat steak and drink fancy bottled water and . . ."

Salty looks in my eyes. I smile, but he doesn't smile back. He groans again, plunking his head down on his paws. I look at Salty's nails. They're *polished*. "Oh, no, they didn't. They gave you a paw-dicure? Oh, buddy, I'm sorry, that just isn't right."

"How do you like our new man?" Will says, coming up next to me. "He's top dog now, huh, a real gov'nor."

I turn around to look at my half brother standing there with that big teasing grin on his face. "Oh, stop with the Dickens' 'gov'nor' stuff," I say. "You agreed to this? Why didn't you stop my mother —"

Will laughs. "He's a *dog*, Willa. He'll get over it."

I hug Salty again. He licks my face, but without his usual enthusiasm. I put my hands on either side of his mouth and try to pull a smile. "Come on, Salty, smile."

He doesn't. They've taken his happy away. I smile at him, trying to cheer him up. "Come on, Salty Dog, give me a grin."

"He doesn't grin," Will says, laughing.

"Stop laughing at me. He does, too."

"Does not," Will says.

"Well, maybe not for *you*, but he smiles at *me*."

Our guest, Mrs. Noonan, is passing by us. She leans in and whispers, "You tell him, honey."

"Okay, I'll bug off," Will says contritely. "I'm sorry, sis." He looks down at my hot-pink sneakers. "Cool shoes."

"Thanks. How was fishing?"

"Listen . . . Willa." Will looks around to be sure no one is listening. He cracks his knuckles, swipes his hand through his sandy-brown hair, sets those sea blue eyes on mine.

"What?" I say.

"I saw him."

"Who?"

"Our father."

A chill runs through my body. "No, Will. You couldn't have. I told you. He's dead. Billy Havisham drowned."

"No, Willa, you're wrong. I saw him out on the Vineyard, in Edgartown, at the docks. I swear I did. I'm sure it was him. He had a fake leg. He was getting in a boat and before I could reach him, he was gone."

"Will . . . it can't be. He crashed into the Atlantic Ocean way down by Washington, DC. Mother showed me the letter from the US Coast Guard. It said, 'We regret to inform you . . .' They searched and dredged the waters for hundreds of miles all up and down the coast. They found some of his clothing, his wallet, and then —"

"I know, I know," Will says. "Part of his leg washed up on a beach."

I grimace at the thought.

"Which proves my point exactly!" Will says, his eyes sparkling with excitement. "They never found his body, did they? People get attacked by sharks and lose arms and legs and survive. I told you, Willa, I saw him yesterday and he had a prosthetic leg. I could tell by the way he was limping across the dock onto his boat."

My head starts to swirl and my stomach does a tailspin. *Oh, my gosh. What if it's true? Yes, a leg washed up onshore. But what if somehow my father survived. . . . Or maybe that wasn't his leg at all. . . . What if . . .*

"Oh, good, Willa, there you are," my mother says, snapping me back to the moment. "Makita called in sick. I need you to serve appetizers later."

"Could I help, too, Ms. Havisham?" Will offers.

Mother smiles. She thinks about it for a few seconds. "You'll need to change," she says. "Do you have a dress shirt and . . ."

"Certainly, Ms. Havisham," he says.

"Stella," she says. "Please call me Stella."

"Very well then, Stella. Don't worry. This Brit bloke cleans up well."

My mother laughs. "All right then, Brit bloke. Cocktails are four to six on the side porch. Willa can fill you in." She looks down, noticing my sneakers. "Where'd you get those?"

"In town, at Lammers'."

"You went *shopping*?" she says incredulously, like I said I went parasailing or skydiving or something.

I roll my eyes. "I wasn't planning to. They just caught my eye."

When my mother leaves, Will turns to me. "Come out to the Vineyard with me tomorrow."

"No, Will."

"Please, Willa. We have to find out."

"No, Will. You've got to stop!" I say this so loudly Salty stands up and barks. He looks at Will, he looks at me. He senses something is wrong.

"Please, Will, you've got to let this rest. You're only going to get hurt again."

"It can't hurt more than his being dead," Will says.

I look out at the front yard, the statue of the girl on her stomach reading a book that Mom and Sam brought me back from their honeymoon trip to Nantucket and then at the cherry tree we planted when Mom and I first moved into the inn. *When life throws you a pit, plant a cherry tree.* I am so lucky. I have a mother, a wonderful stepfather. Will only has two gargoyle-cold grandparents who don't even want him around. . . .

"Never mind," Will says. "I'll go myself."

I feel bad, so sorry for him. "No, Will . . . wait. I'll come, too."

Our guests, particularly the ladies, are quite taken with my brother, Will, during cocktail hour. The Brit bloke looks quite dashing in his tan pants, white collared shirt, and navy blue blazer with his boarding school emblem emblazoned in gold. He pours soda next to my mother, who is opening a bottle of wine. I circulate around with a platter of fresh tomato and pesto bruschetta and grilled shrimp and melon kabobs. I changed into a sundress but am still wearing my hot-pink sneakers, much to my mother's dismay. She'd prefer strappy sandals. At least I'm wearing a dress.

The lowering sun is casting a honey glow over all of us. Mr. Halloran, a lawyer from Syracuse, sits down at the piano just inside the door. He plays "Old Cape Cod" and several of the guests sing along. When Mr. Halloran finishes, Will goes in to the piano. He sits down on the bench, stretches his fingers, cracks his knuckles, and begins to play.

Who knew? Will plays songs from *The Phantom of the Opera* and *Les Misérables* and several other famous musicals, from memory. So my half brother is not only handsome, smart, and rich; he is talented, too. Oh, would Tina and Ruby love to be here right now! Their "boydar" (boy-radar) must be on the blink.

Later, after dinner, up in my room, I text JFK. I tell him how Rosie is leaving and how Mum is coming home. How James Taylor is signing books at Nana's store on Saturday. "You know," I write, "the guy who sings 'You've Got a Friend.'" I tell him about my styling new hot-pink sneakers. I don't tell him about Jess Farrelly's invitation or that Will is on a wild goose chase for our birthfather and that I've agreed to go along.

I go online. I check out the Buoy Boys' home page. Jess, the drummer. Luke LeGraw on guitar and vocals. They're doing an "All Beatles" night at Poppy Marketplace Friday night from seven to nine P.M. All proceeds will benefit the victims of the earthquake in Haiti. *That's really nice of them.* I stare at Jess's picture. Sooo cute. Maybe he was just inviting me to support the cause. How could it hurt to go? *No, Willa, no.* I sign off.

Passing my desk, I pick up the package of book plates Dr. Swammy gave me this afternoon. On impulse I glue one onto the inside front cover of *Kira-Kira* and below the words FROM THE LIBRARY OF, I write *Willa Havisham, Cape Cod, Massachusetts.*

I get into bed, unwrap a taffy, lemon-lime, smiling at the message "Be Happy, Eat Taffy," and begin reading *Kira-Kira.*

I read straight through to the end. I cry when the little sister says how her big sister wanted to live in a house by the sea "because she loved the sea, even though she never saw it."

On the blank page in the front of the book, the one that just has the title *Kira-Kira* on it, I think it's called the half title page, I put today's date and write my review: "Gorgeous, I loved it. What will I remember most? *The love.*"

Speaking of love, I wonder if Dr. Swammy popped the question yet? Oh, I do hope Mrs. Saperstone will say yes. But . . . she has been a widow for so long now. What if she gets cold feet and says no? Oh, no, she must say yes! They are simply perfect for each other.

And I will help them plan a simply perfect Cape Cod wedding.

#

♥ ♥ ♥

CHAPTER 9

To encounter a fine book
and have time to read it
is a wonderful thing.
— Natalie Goldberg

The next day, Wednesday, it's raining. The water is too choppy for Will to take us on his boat out to the Vineyard. Thank goodness. I didn't want to go.

"Tomorrow, for sure," he says.

"Okay," I say, sending up a silent prayer for more rain. I don't want to see my brother hurt again.

After breakfast duty, I curl up with *Ella Enchanted*. It's about a girl who is given a gift from a fairy that turns out to be a curse: Ella must obey any order she is given. Later, on the title page, I write, "I love the main character's spirit!"

I close the book. My mind starts to wander. What is

JFK doing today? Is it raining in Florida, too? I picture Jess, how he looked at me when he asked me to come to his concert. I think he likes me. How do I feel about him? He's just a good friend, that's all. Maybe it wouldn't hurt to go hear him play Friday night. Just as a friend. Just to support the cause. Now, what am I going to wear?

In the afternoon, when the streets have dried, I bike into town. I go back to Lammers', where I found my cool pink sneakers. I buy a jean skirt with pink thread swirls sewn on the back pockets and a pink tank top.

After, I head to the Bramble Library.

Mrs. Saperstone is off today.

"Did she say where she was going?" I ask the other librarian, Ms. Toomajian.

"No, she didn't, Willa, sorry."

"Did she seem particularly happy by any chance?"

"Particularly happy?" Ms. Toomajian laughs. "No more so than usual. Why?"

"Oh . . . no reason." I turn to leave. I bet Dr. Swammy swept Mrs. Saperstone off on a romantic getaway with a picnic basket and champagne, somewhere perfect to present her with that little red book of poems and pop the big question. Maybe he's asking her right now this very second. Oh, say yes, Mrs. S. Say yes!

Two friends from school, Chandler and Caroline, are walking toward me on the street, eating ice cream cones. We stop to chat.

"Everybody's going to Poppy Marketplace Friday night to hear Jess and Luke play," says Chandler.

"You should come with us," Caroline says. "They want everybody from Bramble Academy to come, little kids through high school. It's a fund-raiser for the earthquake victims."

"Who's going?" I say casually, as if this is the first time I'm hearing about it.

"Shefali's coming, Emily, Trish, Kelsie, Greta and Carli, for sure, Lauren, MacKenzie, Allison . . . *everybody*," Chandler says. "We're going to play mini-golf, then get some pizza and sit at the picnic tables in the courtyard to hear the concert."

"And watch the toddlers dance," Caroline says, laughing.

"How come just the little kids dance there?" I say.

"Good question," Chandler says. "I think we ought to bump those babies off the dance floor and show them how it's done."

We laugh.

"When are you going to have another dance party in the barn at your inn?" Caroline asks. "Those were so much fun. It's been a while."

"Yeah, they were great," Chandler says.

"I don't know," I say, "maybe sometime this summer."

"Anyway . . . you should come with us Friday," Caroline says. "It'll be good."

"Maybe," I say, thinking of the new clothes I'm holding in the Lammers' bag. The new outfit I bought for the concert.

Back at the inn, I get out the tray of letters to change the message on the Bramble Board out front. I take the quote I wrote earlier on a slip of paper from my pocket.

> *Everybody can be great, because everybody can serve.*
> — Martin Luther King

I arrange the letters, then step back to read it. I smile. Wait until Mum sees this when she drives back home into town this weekend.

And *What can I do?* I think to myself again.

Books. I want to do something with books. But what?

JFK calls me after dinner. "How's my girl?" he says.
I smile. "Fine, but I miss you."

"Miss you more," he says.

"Really?" I say.

"I sent you that song I wrote for you," he says.

"You're such a good boyfriend," I say. "I can't wait to hear it!"

"I sent it regular mail," he says. "You should get it this weekend."

I look in the mirror. I touch the locket at my neck. "I love you," I say.

"Love you, too," he says. "Hey, and so what's with the mermaid? Did you ever see her?"

It was just before JFK left for Florida that the little tourist girl was insisting she saw a mermaid. JFK, Will, and I were all there together that day on the beach. "No," I say. "I think she swam off. Warmer water, probably, maybe Jamaica."

JFK laughs. "What are you doing for fun? Gotta put those books aside sometimes, you know, give those pretty blue eyes a rest."

My stomach tumbles. I feel confused. *I'm going to a concert Friday. Jess invited me.* "Nothing much.

Mariel's in New York. Ruby and Tina are off stalking lifeguards up and down the Cape."

JFK laughs. "Tina and Ruby. They never change, do they?"

"No, they just get Tina-er and Ruby-er." I think briefly how Ruby used to have a crush on JFK. How she staged this fake contest so that JFK would win Super Bowl tickets to accompany the Sivlers to Florida.

"I heard Luke and Jess are playing at Poppy Marketplace Friday night," JFK says.

My heart beats faster. "Oh, really?"

"Yeah, Luke posted it yesterday. You should go."

"I don't know," I say.

"Our whole class should go support them," JFK says. "They're doing it for charity."

"Yeah, maybe," I say. "I'll think about it. What about you? What are you doing for fun?"

"Running after fly balls, hauling sweaty towels, lugging water jugs. My grandparents take me to dinner at their club every night. The food is awesome but it's so lame there."

"Is that Lorna Doone girl still around?"

JFK laughs. "Her last name isn't Doone, it's Duncan."

"Whatever," I say.

"Yeah, I see her every day at the club. We're the only two people under seventy in the whole place."

My girlfriend radar *beep, beep, beeps.* "What do you mean you see her every day?"

"Our grandparents' favorite tables are right next to each other in the members' dining room. After dinner, Lorna and I hang out in the game room, play pool, or shoot darts until our grandparents finish their after-dinner drinks."

"Oh," I say, feeling queasy. I wait for JFK to say *There's nothing to worry about, Willa. We're just passing the time together. Besides she's ugly and . . .*

"Oh, sorry, Willa," he says. "Gotta go. Gram's calling me. It's surf and turf night at the club. She doesn't want to be late."

When we hang up I am a sea storm of emotions. I don't know whether I'm mostly sad or missing him or mad or jealous or guilty or all of these feelings and more.

Lying on my bed I think about JKF saying how he sits at the table *right next to* Lorna *every night* and how they *hang out in the game room*, the only teenagers in the place, shooting darts and playing pool. I picture Lorna as a gorgeous Taylor Swift–Beyoncé girl leaning across the pool table (*Watch this, Joey*) to make her next shot.

And then my jealousy turns to anger. JFK doesn't have to hang out with a beautiful girl every night. He could tell his grandparents he'd rather take a taxi home. What sort of fool does he think I am? I jump up and open the shopping bag from Lammers'. I try on my new skirt and tank with my pink sneakers. I put on a white hoodie. That looks good. I brush my hair. It's not mermaid length like Tina's and Ruby's but it's getting long. I put on silver hoop earrings. I take off the locket.

At my desk I open my journal and write. The life of Willa Havisham is taking a surprising new direction.

CHAPTER 10

Maybe You Could Adopt Him!

♥ ♥ ♥

Children's books aren't textbooks. Their primary purpose isn't supposed to be "Pick this up and it will teach you this." It's not how literature should be. You probably do learn something from every book you pick up, but it might be simply how to laugh.

— J. K. Rowling

It's Thursday, and as Saturday approaches, and the big braviar wedding Mother is counting on to rekindle her reputation for work-of-art weddings, the tension in the kitchen between Stella and Rosie is thick as pea-soup Cape fog.

"So far I have eighty-nine different miniature cakes," Rosie says to my mother, who is sitting at the table reviewing the menu for the wedding. "I really do need to head up to Hyde Park today. My friend Tara is letting me borrow her car and she's going to watch Lilly for me. I'll be back Friday night. I think maybe I can just alter the decorative frosting on the last eleven a bit, so they look unique, but . . ."

"Absolutely not," Mother says as if Rosie suggested we spike the cakes with arsenic. "Star Bennigan has requested one hundred different cakes and we will not let her down on the most important day of her life. We will not ruin this girl's special day."

I'm at the side counter, slathering butter and minced garlic on the bread to be baked later. I pause with the knife in midair. I bite my tongue. I think that is ridiculous. How could having one hundred different cakes make or break someone's wedding day? How silly. How shallow. This is the side of my mother I just don't respect.

Rosie bursts out in tears. "I'm sorry, Stella. I'm trying my best. I've got so much on my mind. . . ."

"Let it go, Mom, please," I say.

"That's easy for you to say, Willa. You don't have to pay the bills. . . ."

I turn and leave the kitchen so I don't have to listen to her anymore and so I won't say something I will later regret. When my mother leaves, I'll go back and help Rosie finish those last eleven cakes, but right now I can't stand the sight of my mother.

Will is waiting for me outside to boat out to the Vineyard on the wild goose chase for our father. "Ready to go yet?" he says.

"No, Will, I'm sorry, I can't. I've got to help Rosie invent eleven more one-of-a-kind original cakes before my mother chops her head off and dumps her in the chowder."

Will doesn't laugh. He looks hurt. He shrugs his shoulders. "Please yourself."

"Wait, Will, I'm sorry. Maybe tomorrow."

"Yeah, whatever." Off he goes. I feel horrible.

Sam is coming up the steps with a rolled-up mat under his arm, back from his new yoga class. His sister, Ruthie, who was here earlier this summer, inspired him to "make friends with the mat," the yoga mat, that is, and he just registered for a class in Falmouth. Yoga fits Sam's calm, poet-writer-gardener-cook personality perfectly. Sam's already in touch with his "inner OOOOOmmmmm." It's my mother who could really use yoga's purported calming effects.

I give Sam a heads-up on what's going on in the kitchen. Sam smiles. "You've got to love her for caring so much," he says.

"Who?" I say, although I know he's talking about my mother.

"Stella," Sam says. "She didn't want to concern you,

but we're having some cash flow problems; business is down. Stella wants to work harder to bring in more high-end weddings. . . ."

"Braviar weddings," I say. *"Uggh!"*

"Say again?" Sam says, confused.

"Mom's new word for bridezillas," I say. "Never mind. She doesn't have to be so hard on Rosie."

"I know, Willa. It's just your mother's way. She's hard on everybody, especially herself."

"Yeah, whatever," I say, crossing my arms.

"Want to walk with me?" Sam says. "I need to fill the feeders."

The bird feeders, Sam means. "Sure," I say.

As we walk, I think back to the BS days, the "Before Sam" days, about how my mother used to be so incredibly strict with me. She had a rule book as thick as *Moby Dick*, and that has to be the longest book *ever* written. Mom has relaxed and softened up a bit now that she's married to Sam, but she still knows how to drive me crazy.

"Are you still happy here?" I blurt out. "Running the inn?" My heart is beating faster. What if he says no?

"Of course," Sam says. "What makes you ask?" He scoops a green plastic funnel full of seeds and pours them into a tall clear column feeder with tiny holes just the right size for bird beaks, and silver ledges just the right size for birds' claws to clamp on while they are nibbling.

"No reason," I say, shrugging my shoulders. I know Sam's real loves are writing and teaching. He gave up his job teaching English at Bramble Academy to help Mom manage the inn. There would be way more money in that, my mother said. Renovating the inn with expensive designer *everything* was my mother's idea; the only thing I recall Sam being excited about was creating the Labyrinth out back and restoring the flower gardens and vegetable gardens and adding bird feeders, none of which cost very much.

It was Mom who went bonkers spending a fortune on top-of-the-line furniture and window treatments and expensive new china, new silver, new *everything*. No wonder we're having money troubles.

Sam doesn't pry further. He lets me have my mental space. He knows I'll say what's on my mind when I am ready.

"I couldn't be happier," Sam says. "Getting to spend all of this time with my two favorite people on the planet."

"Mom and me?"

"Who else?" Sam says.

"But what about your book, Sam . . . *Dad*?" For Father's Day last month, I told Sam that I was ready to start calling him "Dad," but the old familiar "Sam" still slips out.

"The first time Mom and I had dinner with you, you told us you were working on a book, and I used to see you jotting down notes in that little black notebook you always carried around, but lately, I never hear you mention it."

"All in good time, Willa," he says.

Every once in a while I'll pass by Sam's sunflower-yellow painted office upstairs, the one with the passageway up to the widow's walk, and see him at the old sea captain's desk writing away. If he notices me, he covers up the tablet, which of course makes me even more curious.

"That reminds me," Sam says, "I was in a bookstore over in Brewster yesterday . . ."

"A rival bookstore?" I say. "You better not let Nana get wind of that."

Sam laughs. "You're right about that," he says. "I went to Brewster to check out a chef who might be willing to make a move here and couldn't resist the bookstore. I picked up a slim volume I think you will enjoy. It's called *The Golden Book on Writing*. I'll leave it outside your door."

"Thanks, Dad. That was thoughtful of you. What are *you* reading these days?"

Sam tells me and we finish filling the feeders, then start back inside.

"And what about the baby you and Mom were going to adopt?"

"Whoa, whoa, whoa," Sam says with a laugh. "Who said anything about a baby? Yes, your mother and I were talking about possibly adopting, but we weren't thinking about a baby. There are so many older children who have a much harder chance of ever getting placed in a home. If anything, we'd adopt a child closer to your age so you would have a companion."

"How about Will?" I blurt out. "Maybe you could adopt him!"

Mrs. Noonan is passing by us. She says, "You tell him, honey."

Sam smiles. "Your chaise is all ready by the pond, Mrs. Noonan. I put a reserved sign on it for you."

"Oh, thank you, dear," Mrs. Noonan says.

"One step at a time, Willa," Sam says. "One step at a time. In case you haven't noticed, it's your mom who runs the ship around here. For now, let's see about helping Rosie with those last eleven cakes so she can get on the road. I saw there's a patch of raspberries ready to pick. I bet Rosie can work magic with those."

CHAPTER 11

Just Like a Family

♥ ♥ ♥

'Tis the good reader that makes the good book; . . . in every book he finds passages which seem confidences or asides hidden from all else and unmistakably meant for his ear.
— Ralph Waldo Emerson

When the mail comes, there's a letter from Mariel — a four-page long, handwritten letter — what a lovely thing, like a long lost art form.

Mare is the only teenager I know in America who doesn't have a cell phone.

So far she has been to the Statue of Liberty, the Metropolitan Museum of Art, the American Museum of Natural History, the Guggenheim, the New York Public Library ("There are so many great inexpensive things to do here!"), and friends of her mother's gave them free tickets to two off-Broadway plays and the musical *Wicked* ("It's divine!"). She loves having this time with her mother, but she misses me and Bramble and especially her father and the twins, Nico and Sofia (they got evicted from their crummy motel-room home at the scummy rundown Oceanview Inn, and her dad and the twins are staying with relatives in Springfield, but her father says he had a call from a woman named Mrs. Barrett with an organization called Come Home Cape Cod, and they may be building a house for Mariel's family!). *Oh, how wonderful!* Her father is still insisting that he's going to throw "a proper quinceañera" for Mare when she returns and turns fifteen in August, although "he cannot possibly afford a quince and we both know how I hate to shop. . . . Love you and miss you, till soon, friend. . . . Mariel."

When I finish reading, I decide to reciprocate. A real letter deserves a real letter.

I sit down at my desk, grab a yellow tablet, and start writing, filling Mare in on all that's going on in my life. "Oh, how I wish you were here!"

Later, when I hear Will come home, I go to his room, Captain Ahab. Sam and I named rooms after characters from famous books or authors we particularly like.

I knock and wait.

No answer.

I think about how Captain Ahab was obsessed with finding that great white whale, sort of like how Will is obsessed with finding Billy Havisham.

I knock again, louder this time.

"I'm here," Will says.

I open the door.

Will is looking out the window, his back to me. He doesn't turn around.

"Are you okay?" I say.

He doesn't answer. He doesn't move.

I walk closer until I am standing next to him. I steal a side-glance at his face. There are tears rolling down his cheeks.

"You were right," Will says. "It wasn't him." He makes a whimpering sound, then coughs it off, embarrassed.

"I'm sorry, Will." I reach out to touch his arm. He flinches.

I wrap both arms around him and hug my brother. He doesn't pull away. He shudders, makes a crying sound.

His mother is dead, his father is dead, his grandparents are stone-cold heartless gargoyles who sent him off to boarding school so they wouldn't have to deal with a real-life flesh and blood teenager. I am his only sister, even if I am only a half sister, and right now in this moment, I decide — half or whole, whatever — I'm going to be a better one.

"Come out with me tomorrow night," I say. "A bunch of my friends from school are going out for mini-golf and pizza over at this place called Poppy Marketplace in New Seabury. Our friends, Jess and Luke, have a band called the Buoy Boys and they're playing a benefit concert. It's an all-Beatles tribute."

Will smiles. "In my honor?"

I laugh. "Yes, you got it. They're doing the Beatles in honor of Willa's British brother. See how famous you are?"

"Don't laugh," he says. "When you come visit me at my grandparents' castle one day you'll see just what a gov'nor I am."

"That reminds me," I say. "If Ruby and Tina are at the concert tomorrow night and they ask you about dating a duke's daughter, just go along with it, okay?"

"Not a problem," Will says with a serious expression. "I've dated many a duke's daughter, a few princesses, too."

I laugh.

"My love life is no joking matter," Will says. "You could write a book about it."

Sam knocks on the door. "Dinner, you two."

As we turn to leave, I notice a book on Will's nightstand. I pick it up and read the title. *The Fire-Eaters.* "You like this David Almond guy, huh?"

"Yeah," Will says, "I'm all finished. It's yours now."

Mom, Sam, Will, and I have dinner together on the side porch. Everybody makes small talk. It's pleasant, just like a family. We have mixed fresh greens with balsamic vinaigrette, grilled salmon, red-potato salad, corn on the cob, and strawberry shortcake. Sam has his camera. He asks our night desk manager, Darryl, to take a picture of the four of us.

"Say cheese," Darryl says, and we do. "Nice," Darryl says. "Let me take another just to be sure."

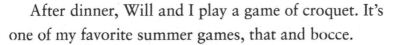

After dinner, Will and I play a game of croquet. It's one of my favorite summer games, that and bocce.

"You're good at this," Will says after I beat him the first time and we start a second round.

"Don't act so surprised," I say, whacking the blue wood ball across the freshly mowed grass, straight through a wicket. *Nice.* "I'm part English, too, don't forget."

Our eyes meet. We're both thinking about our birthfather, but we don't say it.

"Hey, you two," Sam says. He's got his camera again. "Smile!"

"Say cheese," Will whispers to me.

"Cheese," I say, so happy.

When we come in from croquet, Mr. Halloran and Mrs. Noonan and some other guests ask Will if he'll play the piano for them again, and Will quite gallantly acquiesces.

Will suggests we have another piece of that strawberry shortcake, and you never need to invite me twice for shortcake.

"Do you play chess?" Will says as we're rinsing off our dishes.

"Sure," I say. "But prepare to lose at that as well."

"Not possible," Will says. "I'm team captain at Bainbridge."

"Oh, yeah, well. You're in Bramble now, brother."

We go into the game room and sit down at the chess table.

I think of JFK and Lorna in the game room at his grandparents' club in Florida.

Will beats me royally at chess. I face defeat with dignity. "I guess you do have more experience with knights and castles," I say as we walk upstairs to our rooms.

"Mind if I see what my little sister's room looks like? All my girlfriends back in London will want to know, especially the duke's daughter."

I laugh. "Sure, come on in, but I'll warn you. It's really boring."

Will heads straight to my bookcase. "Think you've got enough?" he jokes.

He notices the yellow-topped CHANGE FOR GOOD ✪ jug. "What's that?" he asks.

I explain.

"Make me one," Will says. "I'm bloody loaded with American coins I'll have to toss when I head back home."

My heart clenches. *I don't want you to go.* I have to stop myself from saying, "Wait, no, maybe you can stay here. Maybe Mom and Sam will adopt you," because I know I shouldn't plant false hopes. And I don't even know if Will would want to stay on here in Cape Cod . . . trading a real castle for sand castles.

When Will leaves, I check my cell phone and laptop. No messages from JFK. I could text him, but I don't. He's probably hanging out with the cookie girl.

I look at the outfit I've laid out for tomorrow night.

I look at JFK's picture on my dresser.

I'm just going out with my friends. It's not a date or anything.

I'm glad I thought to invite Will. Now I won't have to show up alone.

In bed I lift the book *Everything on a Waffle* from my nightstand. I read the back cover copy: "Primrose Squarp simply knows her parents did not perish at sea during a terrible storm, but try convincing the other residents of Coal Harbour . . ."

My heart skips a beat. This makes me think of Will, of course. Of how desperately he needs to believe that our birthfather did not perish at sea, that he is somehow still alive and will come back to us. I turn to the first chapter entitled "My Parents Are Lost at Sea" and I dive in, soon hoping for this sweet protagonist Primrose, the same thing I wish for my brother, but it seems much too great a hope for both.

CHAPTER 12

From Cape Cod, With Love

Books were my pass to personal freedom. I learned to read at age three, and soon discovered there was a whole world to conquer that went far beyond our farm in Mississippi.

— Oprah Winfrey

On Friday morning I call Salty and we head to the beach for a walk. I think about what an exciting weekend this is going to be.

Tonight the concert with my friends.

Tomorrow James Taylor is coming to Nana's store.

Sunday Mum is coming to BUC!

Oh, and, of course, there's the braviar Bennigan wedding tomorrow, so Mom will be in full-steam-ahead-super-turbo-Stella mode.

There's a mandatory staff meeting later. Stella will

be barking out orders. Then when she's done, almost as an afterthought as she's standing up to leave, she'll say, "Does anyone have anything to add?"

Recently I suggested some ways the inn could "go green," cutting down on how often we launder towels and linens and replacing all the throwaway plastic water bottles with refillable metal ones. To my mother's credit, she was quite open to the suggestion.

Today, I have a new suggestion. I think it would be nice to put blank journals in each of the rooms like that inn in Vermont Mom and Sam visited when they were researching successful New England inns in preparation for opening ours. The West Mountain Inn it's called. I want to go there someday.

Sam said they put a blank book and pen (and fresh apples and a take-home African violet plant, too, which I think is really, really sweet!) in all the rooms and if guests wish, they can write down what they enjoyed about their visit.

I think it probably makes guests feel like a part of the inn family, a place they want to come back "home" to one day, or maybe even year after year.

I'm not sure what my mom will think of the idea, but I know Sam will love it. I'm pretty certain Rosie and Darryl, Makita and the others will, too.

The beach is empty this early in the morning. The waves lap in and out. I spot a bunch of little sucking black holes in the sand. *Fiddler crabs.* As I walk, breathing in and out, the Willa worries wash away and my mind is a fresh, clear slate.

It's in moments like this, when I least expect it, that some of my best ideas come.

And so *what can I do?*

I pick up my pace. I breathe in and out. I want to do something nice for the planet . . . something that involves books. I think about finding that book belonging to that girl from Atlanta. I noticed it wasn't on the stairs today. I wonder who's enjoying it now.

I think of my books. How I told Dr. Swammy that I don't lend them out because they are my favorite possessions and . . .

Give them away, from Willa, with love.

What?

I stop walking. I feel a spark of excitement.

Give them away, from Willa, with love.

These are my words, my own voice inside me.

My books? Give my books away? All of my beautiful, wonderful books? Many given as gifts from the people I love? Most with my thoughts scribbled throughout . . . a lasting record of how I felt at eight and nine and ten and eleven and twelve and thirteen and fourteen and . . . ?

Think of it as planting a garden, Willa.

There it is again, my voice inside me. Ideas are spark-spark-sparking in my head.

"Come on, Salty. Let's run!"

I need to get home to my desk where there's paper so I can get all of this down.

Back at the inn, I rush up to my room. I sit at my desk, sweating, heart pounding, pull out a yellow tablet, grab a pen. I notice the package of book plates Dr. Swammy said people use when they loan out books. I look at my bookcase, filled two books deep, top to bottom with all the great books I've read. And then I picture all the other books out in our library downstairs. They do look pretty sitting on the shelves. But books aren't pretty objects to be looked at. Yes, the covers are lovely, but it's the words inside that count. No book gets read sitting closed on a shelf collecting dust. Books are living things; they call out for people to communicate with them — to read them —

and question them and laugh with them and cry with them. . . .

I think about how moved I was reading that *Three Cups of Tea* book. I would send those children my books, but all of my books are in English and how would I . . .

Think simple, Willa. Start small.

I picture the bumper sticker I see on cars around town: THINK GLOBAL, ACT LOCAL.

My local is Cape Cod. Every summer, people from all over the country, from all over the world, maybe, come to visit our little sandy wonderland.

I think of the girl from Atlanta who left her book on the beach. Maybe she did so intentionally! Maybe she wanted to pass it on! I picture the young tourist girl who thought she saw the mermaid. How sad she must have been leaving Cape Cod, crossing back over that roller-coaster bridge to the mainland from her vacation. I imagine her sitting in the backseat of her parents' minivan, taking one last look down at the waves of the Cape Cod Canal. But, then, what if she remembered that treasure she found . . . maybe on a bench on Main Street. She glances down at her lap, at the book she is holding. It's *The BFG*, by Roald Dahl . . . my copy of *The BFG*. She opens the cover and reads aloud the book plate:

Take me home, free, if you wish to read,
Then, when you are finished, replant the seed.
Leave me somewhere for a new friend to find.
A book is a perennial thing,
It blooms on and on and on.
From Cape Cod, With Love
Willa Havisham

I stop writing. My hand is shaking. I start to laugh. I feel a sizzle of happiness. I love this idea. *What can I do?* I think I know now. I think this is it!

But . . . first I should probably get another opinion. Who should I talk to?

Mrs. Saperstone, of course.

She'll tell me what she thinks.

CHAPTER 13

Building Customer Loyalty

♥ ♥ ♥

*One of the books I really loved, at the fairly advanced age
of fourteen, was Louisa May Alcott's Little Women. I was
staying at my grandmother's house, with a lot of cousins
around, and I didn't want anyone to know — so I kept it a
secret. . . . I found it absolutely captivating.*
— Tracy Kidder

Mrs. Saperstone is sitting on a bench beneath a tree
in the readers' garden behind the library, enjoying her
lunch. When she sees me, her face brightens.

"Willa!" she calls excitedly. "I wanted you to be the
first to know, but I think maybe you already do. Ms.
Toomajian said you —"

"Did you say *yes*?" I ask, holding both hands, fingers crossed, above my head.

"Of course," she says, laughing. "I just wondered
what took him so long."

"Whoo-hoo!" I shout, rushing to hug her. Her eyes

fill with tears. Mine do, too. We do a little happy dance in front of the whale spoutin' fountain.

Mrs. Saperstone wipes her face and blows her nose. "After my husband, Gary, died, Willa, I thought for sure I would spend my life alone. Filled with my work and friends, and *books*, certainly, but . . ."

"I know," I say. "I know what you mean."

Mrs. Saperstone laughs. "You have such an old soul in that young body, Willa."

"I know," I say. "Have you set a date?"

"Not yet," she says. "We wanted to wait and speak with Mum on Sunday and then we need to make an appointment with this very famous wedding planner we've been hearing about."

"My mother?" I say.

"No, dear girl," she says, with a smile. "*You*, of course!"

My heart bubbles bright. "Well, I thought you'd never ask! I'd be honored."

"The only thing is, Willa," Mrs. Saperstone says, "we want our wedding to be simple. We need it to be modest. On a teacher's and librarian's salaries —"

"I understand," I say. "I planned Nana and Gramp Tweed's wedding and it was very economical. And just this summer, I planned my aunt Ruthie's wedding at the inn and . . ."

"Oh, no," Mrs. Saperstone says. "I highly doubt we can afford the Bramblebriar. Just yesterday I overheard some patrons talking about the Bennigan affair your mother is planning. . . ."

"That's my mother's way of doing things," I say. "I am the wedding planner's *daughter*, and I have my own new style."

Mrs. Saperstone nods down at my sneakers. "Yes," she says. "I noticed."

I tell Mrs. Saperstone about my idea for leaving my books in public places where people can take them for free and then pass them along when they are done. I tell her the little poem I thought up to write on the book plates inside. "What do you think?" I say.

"I LOVE IT!" she says. "That's what I think. It's a perfectly marvelous idea. You'll be like the Johnny Appleseed of books except instead of planting apple seeds —"

"We'll be planting books!" I finish.

"But will you give them all away, Willa? Even your favorites? *Little Women* and *Anne of Green Gables* . . ."

"Yes," I say, "all of them."

"From Cape Cod, With Love," Mrs. Saperstone says. "I love it. Have you told Dr. Swaminathan yet?"

"No, you're the first," I say.

"Well, then, I'm doubly delighted," Mrs. S. says.

A red bird lands on the whale spoutin' fountain. I smile. *Hi, Gramp.*

"I would have told my idea to Gramp Tweed first, of course," I say, looking at the red bird. "He was the one who first got me started reading 'the good ones,' but now you and Dr. S. keep it going."

The red bird tilts its head my way and then flies off.

I love you, Gramp.

Love you, too, Willa.

"Come inside for a second, Willa," Mrs. Saperstone says, standing up and collecting her lunch things. "I've got some books for you."

"Now we're talking," I say, and she laughs.

Inside the library, Mrs. Saperstone hands me *Firegirl* by Tony Abbott, *Among the Hidden* by Margaret Peterson Haddix, and *Make Lemonade* by Virginia Euwer Wolff.

"I remembered how much you loved Wolff's *True Believer*," Mrs. Saperstone says. "And I've met those other two authors at librarian events. I think you'll enjoy their work."

"Thanks, Mrs. S.," I say, turning to leave.

"Oh, Willa," she calls to me.

"Yes?"

"Don't forget. Those are library books. Don't go writing in those or giving them away."

I laugh and she laughs. "Of course not," I say. "Don't worry."

♥   ♥   ♥

At the staff meeting, I make my suggestion about putting blank books in the guest room as another way of "building customer loyalty." I add that last bit to appease my mother's business sensibilities.

"I like it," Sam says nicely, but not too enthusiastically. He knows my mother won't approve if she feels we are ganging up on her.

Mother rolls her eyes. "How much will they cost?"

"You can buy blank journals at the dollar store," I say.

"But are they cheap-looking?" Mother says, crinkling her eyebrows.

There she goes. On one hand she's worried about finances, but on the other hand she insists on only the fanciest, most expensive stuff.

"Mom, I think we can do 'top-shelf' without 'top dollar.'"

Sam clears his throat. I catch a quick wink and he purses his lips not to smile.

My mother does not look convinced.

"I will choose journals with nice covers," I say.

"Besides, it's what people will write inside that counts. Just think of all the nice things our guests will say about the inn and the service and the food and the grounds and the weddings, of course, *especially* the weddings."

Sam winks at me.

My mother raises her chin. "I guess we can give it a try," she concedes.

"Great, Mom, thanks. Oh . . . and . . . one of my friends from school was asking when we were going to have another dance party in the barn —"

"It's booked all summer," Mother says, cutting me off before I can finish my thought, "with rehearsal dinners and private parties."

"Well, then, maybe in the fall," Sam says, "when school starts up again. A Halloween party for sure. Don't you think, Stella?"

"We'll see," my mother says.

I follow Sam out of the meeting. We walk to the vegetable garden where I help him pick lettuce and tomatoes for tonight's dinner. I tell him about my new idea to leave my books in public places for others to find and enjoy.

Sam wipes sweat from his forehead and smiles. "Now that's what I call community rent," he says. "Just think how far those books might go. Across the country, around the world. Just imagine all the different people you will be connecting."

"I hadn't thought about it that way," I say. "But that's nice."

Sam pats my cheek. His eyes meet mine. "I am so proud you're my daughter."

The word *daughter* makes me feel good.

"Thanks, Dad," I say. "I'm proud of you, too. You're the one who taught me about 'community rent.' You and Mum, that is."

"And don't forget your mother," Sam says. "Think of all the charity races she sponsors and runs in. She personally raised five thousand dollars for that Race for the Cure she ran in last year. She just doesn't make a big deal about it."

"Why is Mom so especially mean, I mean *cranky,* lately?" I say.

"Stella's the bottom-line, checks-and-balances part of our team," Sam says.

Team. I like that. That's right. We're a team.

"She wants to make sure the Bramblebriar keeps thriving," Sam says. "There are businesses closing all over the place. Stella's determined to see us through."

We move over to the squash section and gather fat green zucchini for those spicy raisin-nut cookies we always have in the jar this time of year. You wouldn't think this funny-looking vegetable . . . or is it a fruit? . . . would make such moist and yummy cookies, but they do! Yum, yum, yum.

When Sam and I go inside, I set off to find Will. I'm excited to tell him about my ideas to put journals in the rooms and to leave free books for tourists to find.

I ask around, but no one has seen him. Finally, Darryl, our night desk manager, says, "He left early this morning, Willa. He said to tell you he heard a relative was on Cape, and he was headed up to Yarmouth to find him."

My heart sinks. I groan. *Oh, no, Will, not another goose chase.* I wish there was some way I could stop him, to prevent him from having more disappointment and pain. Our birthfather is dead. It's sad, but true. Why can't Will accept that?

Up in my room, I lie down on my bed and begin reading *Make Lemonade*:

> *"I am telling you this just the way it went*
> *with all the details I remember as they were,*
> *and including the parts I'm not sure about."*

Hmm . . . I love the main character, LaVaughn.
It's like she's right here talking to me.

So much to write in my journal. About how worried I am about Will. How excited I am for Mrs. S. and
Dr. Swammy. How can I make their wedding perfect?
Top-shelf without being top dollar? Ideas start to flow
and I grab a yellow tablet to catch them quick.

CHAPTER 14

Poppy Marketplace

♥ ♥ ♥

*Books . . . are like lobster shells. We surround ourselves
with 'em, then we grow out of 'em and leave 'em behind,
as evidence of our earlier stages of development.*
— Dorothy Sayers

I was right. It wasn't Billy Havisham. I feel so bad
for Will. I start asking him a bunch of questions, but
he says, "Just drop it, okay?" so I do.

I check my phone. No message from JFK. I could text
him, but I need to get ready for the concert. I feel a jolt of
excitement when I think about Jess. What is wrong with
me? JFK . . . Jess . . . JFK . . . Jess . . . I feel so confused.

I shower, then dry my hair, brushing one side down
straight and putting some gel on the other side to
crunch up soft curls — "the Willa" style Ruby designed
for me. The one and only time Ruby and I felt like
friends. That girl and I just do not connect.

My new pink outfit looks good. I put on some makeup
and perfume. I look at JFK's picture on my dresser.

Where are you right now? Why haven't you called me? Are you at the club with Lorna right now? I stare at my face in the mirror. I think about Jess, his laid-back manner, his beautiful brown eyes and quiet laugh . . . how nice he is . . . how he seems so really into me.

I put on my favorite silver earrings. I don't wear the silver locket.

♥ ♥ ♥

It's about six o'clock when Will and I get to the grouping of gray clapboard buildings with crushed shell pathways called "Popponesset Marketplace." There's the old familiar blackboard with CONCERT TONITE, 7-9 P.M. printed in bright yellow chalk.

When I was little and came each summer to visit Nana in Bramble, she would bring me here for the free concerts on summer weekend nights. She'd spoil me rotten at Carol's Toy Store and then we'd check out the tourist shops, get cones from Ben & Jerry's, and listen to the band. Sometimes Nana would dance with me.

There's the candy store, Country Store, the art gallery, pizza and smoothies places, and, of course, Bobby's Raw Bar, packed with customers. Sometimes Mom and Sam and I come here to the dining area out behind Bobby's Raw Bar for the hands-down best lobsta' roll on Cape. That lobsta' roll is legendary — huge and fresh. "A feast for a king," Sam says. They serve great chowda', too. Ahhh . . .

In case you haven't noticed, we drop "er" to "a" when we're talking about the seafood we love so much around here. . . . Say "lobtsa'" and "chowda'" and you might pass for a local and not a tourist. . . . Not that we don't love tourists . . . we do!

Several friends from school are already playing mini-golf. I introduce Will to Greta and Carli, who are also just arriving, and the four of us team up for a game.

I hear an unmistakable laugh and then a copycat one and I look over across the pathway to the back nine and, sure enough, there are Ruby and Tina. They are flirting with two older guys, college-aged; my guess would be lifeguards they met conducting research for their "book."

Tina spots us and nudges Ruby and they both wave and shout, "Hey, Will!"

How about "Hey, Willa"? What am I, invisible?

Will smiles and waves back. "Tina's cute," he says.

"You like her?" I ask.

"She's pretty," he says. "And fun. But that other one . . ."

"Ruby?"

"Right. Ruby. She's cute, too, but way too much of a headache."

I laugh. "Remember. If you get cornered by Ruby, mention the duke's daughter."

"What? Oh, oh, right. The duke's daughter."

"Come on," I say, "I don't want them to think I was lying."

"No worries, sister," he says, laughing. "I've got your back."

"*I've got your back?*" I smile. "Since when did you start sounding so American?"

"Since I've got American family," he says.

♥   ♥   ♥

When we finish playing golf, we walk to the pizza place and order slices. I hear the sound of a guitar and someone on a mike: "check, check." My heart jumps.

Luke and Jess.

"Those your friends?" Will asks.

"Yep."

"They better do justice to my homeboys," Will says, and I crack up laughing.

"*Homeboys?*"

"You know, John . . . Paul . . . Ringo," he says.

"Yes," I say, laughing. "The Beatles, I got it."

We take our pizza out into the crowded court-yard and nudge our way to sit on top of a picnic table next to a family with three little blond-haired boys, all wearing matching blue polo shirts. The place is buzz-ing with people of all ages, eating dinner, talking, laughing, suntanned and relaxed in sundresses, shorts, and colorful T-shirts. . . . Fathers dashing after giggling runaway toddlers . . . mothers wiping dribbles from chins . . . grandparents doling out dollars for treats . . . kids wearing glow-in-the-dark necklaces with a cone in one hand and a brown bag filled with candy in the other.

This is Poppy Marketplace. Cape Cod at its finest.

There's background radio music playing in advance of the Buoy Boys, and already a slew of toddlers are up on the dance floor, little butts out, heads bopping, dancing around like a bunch of ducks. Some young mothers are holding their babies, swaying back and forth. An adorable little boy with blue and white striped pants and a matching baseball cap bends down and scoops up some crushed shells in his hands and throws them at his mother. Giggling, he runs off fast as a bandit, she running fast behind.

When I see Jess sit down at the drums, a fluttery feeling runs all through me. I try not to watch him, but he looks so . . . so . . . like a hot drummer in a rock band, which, of course, he is. Way cuter than those pictures of Ringo Starr.

Tina and Ruby make their way toward us and find spots on the bench seat.

"He's so cute, isn't he, Willa?" Carli says, noticing me noticing Jess.

"Who?" I say, taking a bite of my pizza.

"Jess, *duh*. You're staring at him."

My face reddens. I take another bite of pizza.

Tina is staring at me. She heard Carli asking me about Jessie. I try to avoid her glare, but Tina is relentless. She walks to me, staring, staring, until her face is just inches from mine.

"What?" I say, finally give in.

"Come here," she says, grabbing my hand and dragging me around the side of the building by the restrooms, out of earshot from our friends. *"You like him, don't you?"* she says, eyes big as Bambi's.

"Who?"

"Oh, spare me, Willa. . . . *Jess*, of course."

"No," I say weakly.

"Look at you," Tina says. "Your face turned red as a fire engine as soon as Carli mentioned Jessie's name."

"I'm sunburned," I say.

Tina smiles, clearly loving this. She squints her eyes and checks me out from head to toe. "Look at how nicely you did your hair and makeup, too. You? Makeup? And check out the new pink outfit and sneakers — they're really cute by the way — where'd you buy them?"

I shrug my shoulders. "No big deal. So what, I went shopping."

"*You*, shopping? Come on, Willa. It's me, Tina . . . remember? You never go shopping. You hate to shop." She flings her blond hair over her shoulder, case closed.

It's me, Tina, remember? I remember. You were my best friend. You knew me better than anyone. How did we drift so far . . .

"Oh, my gosh," Tina shrieks. She's staring at my throat. She reaches to check around my neck. "Where's JFK's locket?"

"I don't know. I don't always wear it."

"Yes, you do, Willa. You always do!"

The Buoy Boys' first Beatles number, "Love Me Do," cuts loudly through the night air. All of a sudden, I feel horrible. I know perfectly well that I'm not wearing JFK's locket. I love him, but I can't stop thinking about Jess, too. I bite my lip to keep from crying.

"Willa, honey, it's okay," Tina says sweetly, just like our BFF days. She pats her hand on my back and smiles. "So what, you like Jess. Good for you. It's not like you're married to Joey. It's summertime. Have some fun.

Don't worry about it. You worry so much you're going to grow worrywarts all over that pretty face and . . ."

I start to laugh. I hug her. "Please don't say anything."

She puts her fingers to her lips, motioning that she's zipping them. She reaches out her perfectly manicured fingers to fix a stray strand of my hair. "Your hair's looking really good, by the way. I like it long."

We smile at each other. Good old Tina. I miss her. I miss hearing how she sees the world. We used to tell each other everything, especially when it came to liking boys. I remember back when we used to spy on my mother's weddings, even with binoculars sometimes, scouting out the cutest guys at the receptions. We had fun together. I miss all the fun we had.

"Lighten up, Willa," Tina says. "It's good to date other guys. Joey's the one and only boy you've ever even kissed."

"I know, but I feel like I'm betraying him."

"Who knows what he's doing in Florida all summer," Tina says. "You aren't *married*. You're only fifteen."

"Fourteen and a half," I correct her.

"I know, I know," Tina says, rolling her eyes. "I always like to round up."

I giggle. "How old have you been telling those college lifeguards you are?"

"Eighteen," she says, and we laugh.

"Well, you could certainly pass for it," I say.

"Thanks, Willa," Tina says, reaching into her pocket for lip gloss. "And I mean it. Don't make this into a big deal. Yeah, you've got Joey's locket, but it's not a diamond ring. We're in *high school*, Willa. We're supposed to date different people. How else will you know if you've found 'the one' if you've only ever dated *one*?"

Tina is making surprisingly good sense. But even though I haven't even gone on a date with Jess, it still feels like I'm cheating on JFK.

I nod my head. "Thanks, Tina."

"Anytime," she says. "Oh, and . . . I like your brother. Really, really. I know Ruby does, too, but . . ."

"He likes you, too," I say.

"Truly?" Tina says.

"That's what he said."

Tina hugs me. "Let's go, then, silly. We've got cute boys waiting on us."

Another song starts up. "I Want to Hold Your Hand."

"That's got a good beat," Tina says, yanking my hand to hurry me along. "Come on, Willa. Let's show those babies how to dance and get this party started."

CHAPTER 15

The After-Beatles Beach Party

♥ ♥ ♥

There is more treasure in books than in all the pirates' loot on Treasure Island . . . and best of all, you can enjoy these riches every day of your life.
— Walt Disney

All the while I'm dancing to Beatles tunes with Tina and the toddlers and my friends, I keep stealing looks at Jess. He makes a very good Beatle. He looks so cute in that simple white tee and cutoff jean shorts, that leather rope choker around his neck. Every time his eyes meet mine, I feel a flutter of butterflies inside.

They play a slower set: "Hey Jude" . . . "Eleanor Rigby" . . . "Yesterday" . . . and then the beautiful song "In My Life," one of the most popular "first dance" numbers for the bride and groom at weddings. It's about how you might know and love a lot of people in your life, but out of all of them, you love your sweetheart *more*. Isn't that so romantic?

♥   ♥   ♥

The Bouys are a huge hit with the entire Poppy Market crowd . . . or maybe it's just because everybody likes the Beatles. Old people, young people, we all know the songs.

A lady takes the microphone and announces that this is a benefit concert for the victims of the earthquake in Haiti. She directs people toward two tables where volunteers are accepting donations and urges us to "be as generous as possible."

She turns and nods, smiling at Jess and Luke. "And please note that these two talented young men from Bramble Academy have very kindly donated their time here, directing the payment they would have received toward supporting tonight's cause."

There is a spontaneous applause. Luke takes a flashy, funny, dramatic bow. Jess seems embarrassed by the praise, hunkering down out of the limelight. Finally, he nods his head and waves a drumstick briefly to acknowledge the audience.

He's modest. I like that.

Tina looks at me and winks and then redirects her attention back to my brother. Toward the end of the last set, many of the families with young children mill off toward home and the dance floor is clearer for the rest of us. When the Buoys play "Paperback Writer" I check Jess's eye and he nods at me.

Is he playing that because he knows I want to be a writer?

I look at him again and he smiles.

Will and Tina are sitting on top of a picnic table talking. Will says something and Tina throws her head back, laughing. Will looks happy. I am happy for him. He's fitting in so nicely with my group of friends. No surprise. He is, after all, a really great guy.

Ruby is over in front of the art gallery talking with an older dude, definitely a lifeguard. Every once in a while I see her checking out Will and Tina, but it's clear to all that Will and Tina are hitting it off, big-time, and Ruby is respecting that. Ruby is never one to let another girl stand in her way of a boy, but Tina is Ruby's best friend after all. I feel a pang of jealousy. I think about Mariel in Manhattan. I wish that she were here. But then again, I felt so close to Tina earlier tonight . . . just like old times.

Can a girl have more than one *best* friend?

Tina bursts out laughing. Will is waving his hands in the air, reenacting some funny story or other, and Tina is glowing in his company. They seem so good together. Wow . . . what if Tina and Will become a couple and stay together? Tina might just be my sister-in-law one day!

Reason: Enough, Willa, enough, you're getting way ahead of yourself.

Willa: I know, I know, but it could happen.

The Buoys finish playing at nine with a really sweet version of "Let It Be," Luke smooth on the vocals, Jess's eyes closed, head swaying back and forth as if he's *feeling* the words of the song. There is something about that boy, something so . . .

"Are you coming to the beach?" Carli asks me. "A bunch of us are going." She looks at Jess and smiles. I think Carli has a crush on him, too. "It's an after-Beatles beach party," she says.

The pizza shop is closing. The lady in the clothing store turns her sign to read OPEN AT 10 A.M. I look over at Jess breaking down their sound system.

"Sure," I say, "I'm in. I'll meet you there."

My pink sneakers lead me across the crushed gray and white shells to Jess. He's leaning over, unplugging wires. "Great concert," I say.

"Willa," he says. "Hey. I didn't think you were coming tonight."

"Coming to the beach, Jess and Willa?" Tina shouts this as she and Will pass by, too focused on each other to stop and wait for an answer.

Thank goodness it's dark so Jess can't see me blushing.

"You going?" he asks me in that dreamy low voice.

I look at him, blue eyes to brown, and I have no other answer but yes.

Luke's father arrives with his SUV to take the equipment home.

"Keep my drums till tomorrow?" Jess asks Luke.

"Sure, dude," Luke says. "Later."

"Oh, boys . . . I'm glad you're still here," says the lady who runs the Marketplace. "We tabulated the checks and cash and credit card donations and it is just astounding, the generosity of Poppy patrons. We raised more than three thousand dollars this evening."

"Good people," Jess says.

"Good band," I say.

Jess smiles at me. He looks down at my sneakers, notices my new outfit.

"You look pretty in pink," he says.

Jess and I walk across the road, across the parking lot, through the grounds of the Popponesset Inn toward the beach where our friends are. We don't talk, but there's something screaming between us. We pass by the tent where there's a wedding reception going on. I think briefly how tomorrow is my mother's debut-return to her "braviar days."

At the top of the beach stairs, the night breeze hits my face.

There's our crowd over there to the right. They have built a bonfire. Somebody brought music. That looks like Will and Tina standing down by the water's edge, and that is unmistakably Ruby sitting up on that life-guard throne, queen of everything.

I steal a side-glance at Jess in the moonlight. I smell cologne and sweat and the sea. He looks wild and distant and dreamy, like Heathcliff in *Wuthering Heights*.

"I'm glad you came out," he says.

"Me, too," I say.

"I've wanted to ask you out for at least two years now," he says.

"Really?" My heart is pounding like a drum. "Why didn't . . ."

"You know why," he says.

JFK. He and JFK are good friends.

"You don't hit on your friend's girl," he says.

And so Jess is handsome and sweet and civic-minded

114

and has integrity, too. *Oh, this isn't good, Willa. This isn't good at all.*

"I'm sorry," Jess says. "I tried staying away, but . . ."

"Let's walk," I say.

"K," he says.

At the bottom of the beach stairs, there is no hesitation, no indecision.

There are two choices, walk right to our friends or walk left.

We turn left and head out along the deserted beach, barely lit by stars.

We don't talk, we just walk, that "something" still screaming between us.

 "You've Got a Friend"

♥ ♥ ♥

What one reads becomes part of what one sees and feels.
— Ralph Ellison

"Let's go, let's go, up and at 'em, Willa!" My mother is knocking at my door.

I look at the clock. Seven thirty. Saturday morning. I can't believe I overslept. "Coming, Mom."

Stella wanted everyone not on the breakfast shift to report to the staff room at seven to go over, for the gazillionth time, all the details of today's Bennigan wedding. The ceremony will be at five at the gazebo by the pond, followed by the reception.

I rush to get dressed. I stop when I remember.

Last night. The walk with Jess on the beach.

How the very moment we were out of sight from our friends, we had turned and kissed each other.

I stare at my face in the mirror. I don't look at the picture of JFK. My eyes rest on the silver locket. The one I didn't wear last night.

"Willa, *now!*" my mother shouts, and I rush to get my orders.

Tina texts me, asking where I was last night. She noticed Jess didn't show up at the party, either. "Details," she demands, "now."

I quickly text her back. "I went home, didn't feel well."

"Oooh, poor baby," she replies. "See ya at Sweet B at 2!"

James Taylor, signing at Sweet Bramble Books. I didn't know Tina liked his music.

Will looks cheerful as can be at the staff meeting.

"So you're into Tina, huh?" I say.

"You could say that," he says. "Where did you go last night?"

"Home. I didn't feel well. Too much pizza." Another lie slips easily off my tongue.

"Back to Tina," he says. "Is she tight with anybody?"

"Yes, *you*," I say. "I think you're going to have to break that poor duke's daughter's heart."

"That's what they call me all throughout the UK," Will says.

"What's that?" I say, taking the bait.

"Havisham the Heartbreaker."

I roll my eyes. Will laughs. "No, really, they do."

I think about "heartbreaker," how it applies to me.

Me, Jess, JFK. Who'll be the one with the broken heart?

After lunch, Will and I bike to Sweet Bramble Books for the big event. There's already a line out the door and down the street, excited fans waiting to meet James Taylor — and buy lots of Nana's books, I hope.

We park our bikes. "Come on," I say to Will, and we make our way into the store.

Tina and Ruby are standing right next to the table where the famous singer is autographing books. As I get closer I hear a lady, probably Mr. Taylor's publicist, asking Nana to please "move those two girls along now."

"What's going on?" I ask Tina.

I notice Ruby is holding their *Beach Boys of Cape Cod* album-book.

"We thought maybe JT could help us get our book published!" Tina says.

"*JT?*" I repeat.

Ruby rolls her eyes. "Yes, Willa. Don't you know anything?"

"Yes, Ruby, I do. I know it's rude to stalk an author, trying to pitch your own book idea."

"It's not an *idea*, Willa," Ruby says, red hair flipped back, one hand on her hip. "It's a *book*. And we're not stalking. We're talking. That's all. She smiles her most engaging Ruby smile, shining her perfect white teeth toward "JT."

Mr. Taylor looks over at us and smiles. He chuckles. He's enjoying this.

His publicist, or whoever she is, is clearly not amused. She leans down to whisper something in the singer's ear.

Mr. Taylor shakes his head. "No, it's okay, they're fine."

"We've got a friend in you, right, JT?" Ruby says, reveling in her Ruby-esque, unabashed self-promotion.

Mr. Taylor laughs and shakes his head, looking up to greet the next person in line.

Tina walks over to Will. He says something and Tina giggles.

"Mr. Taylor," Nana says, "let me introduce my granddaughter, Willa Havisham."

"Pleasure to meet you, Willa," the famous singer says, reaching out to shake my hand warmly.

"Thank you so much for coming to our store," I say.

"Shall I sign one for you?" he asks.

"Absolutely," Nana says. "You should see this girl's collection of books. All she does is read, read, read."

I smile inside, thinking to myself, *Well, that's not all I do.*

"She's going to be a famous author one day, Mr. Taylor," Nana brags on. "Just you wait and see."

"Good for you," Mr. Taylor says to me. He scrawls *Write your heart out, Willa,* and then signs his name. He hands me the book and smiles.

What a nice man, so humble despite his fame (Ruby could take a lesson from that!) and funny and *handsome,* an attribute not lost on the crowd of ladies waiting with cameras for their brief moments with the star.

I turn to look. Will and Tina are gone.

"It was nice to see Tina again," Nana says. "She hasn't been around in a while."

"Oh, you'll be seeing more of her now," I say, "now that she's an aspiring author and has a huge crush on Will."

I think back to how Nana would always insist I take a bag of candy for my "best friend" Tina whenever I came for my new supply of sweets.

"Tina had a great new idea for saltwater taffy flavors," Nana says. "A summer-beach line targeted especially for teenagers . . ."

I think of two teenagers on the beach last night.

"Coconut Oil . . . Toasted Marshmallow . . . Chocolate Kisses . . ."

I think of kissing Jess, how nice it was. How very confused I am.

Back at the inn, I shower and change into a nice dress for the Bennigan wedding. I force my feet into sandals despite the fact they are shouting, *"Pink sneakers, please."*

As I pass by the kitchen on my way out to the gazebo, I see Rosie hugging Darryl, then Makita. I walk toward them. They are brushing tears away.

"Please don't tell Stella yet, Willa," Rosie says. "She needs to be focused on the wedding today, but I found a perfect apartment for me and Lilly right near the school. I signed the lease and I'm anxious to get settled. . . ."

"Oh, Rosie," I say, my heart half-and-half, sad-happy for her.

She smiles at me. "It's just the perfect place for us."

"When?" I say.

"Tomorrow," she says.

"*Tomorrow?*" I say.

"Yes. This is hard and I don't want to drag it out. I've told Sam and he's okay with it. He thinks he may have found somebody to replace me, a baker from a place he likes up in P'town."

"Good for you, Rosie," I say, giving her a hug. "We'll miss you, but maybe you'll come back to work here. . . ."

"That's right," Rosie says. "Maybe I'll be back when I graduate. Lord knows there's lots of good restaurants on Cape Cod. And Lilly and I will be back to visit often. We're not going that far away."

"Friends forever," I say.

Rosie nods. Then a look of fear passes over her face.

"Don't worry about my mother," I say. "Her bark is worse than her bite."

Salty pad, pad, pads into the kitchen, barks hello, and licks my hand.

Rosie and I laugh. "You're so smart, Salty," she says.

"And he smiles, too," I say. "Watch."

"Smile, Salty, smile."

Rosie and I wait.

Salty shows his stuff.

"That's right," I say, wrapping my arms around his thick, warm, golden neck. Who cares if he makes my sundress smell like fish? "That's my Salty Dog!"

CHAPTER 17

Like a Washing Machine

♥ ♥ ♥

*Read the great stuff but read the stuff that isn't so great,
too. Great stuff is very discouraging. If you read only
Beckett and Chekhov, you'll go away and only deliver
telegrams for Western Union.*
— Edward Albee

When my duties for the wedding are over, I
head back up to the main house to change. I keep picturing my mother's face deftly overseeing each note
of the Bennigan affair as if conducting an orchestra.
The service, the setting, the flowers, the music, the
menu . . . the one hundred unique cakes displayed, waiting to be served. . . . Everything perfect. Guests gushing
with praise. World-renowned wedding planner Stella
Havisham, jubilant, her crown as Queen of the Braviars
now back securely on her beautiful ebony head.

I think over some ideas I have for Mrs. Saperstone
and Dr. S.'s wedding. There has to be something special involving books since both of them are such huge

book lovers. And as for food . . . I'm thinking about asking some of the restaurants on Main Street to each send a platter of fancy hors d'oeuvres with book-related names — and maybe ask the guests to vote for their favorites and then I could send a write-up about it to the local newspaper. . . .

I go out to check the mailbox.

There's an oversize envelope addressed to me.

The handwriting is JFK's, the return address, Florida. My heart begins pounding. I race up to my room, Salty Dog right behind me.

I close my door, plop on my bed, and tear open the envelope.

There's no note, just his writing on the clear case covering the disc.

For My Girl
Love, Joey

A cry catches in my throat. Salty's ears perk up. He looks at me. I pop in the song and we listen.

From the first line, I am crying. In minutes, I am sobbing.

Salty Dog barks, worried for me.

The song is beautiful. And the lyrics are *good*.

Does he really mean all of those things about me?

My mind flashes to last night on the beach with Jess.

"For my girl, love, Joey."

Oh, JFK, I'm sorry.

Salty tilts his head at me.

I play the song again. I sob some more. I rush for my phone and text him.

"I love it!" I write.

I wait. No response. He must have his phone off. I wish I had his grandparents' number. Wait, I know. . . .

I hurry downstairs for a phone book, find the Kennellys' number, and dial.

JFK's mother answers and gives me the Florida number.

"Please ask him to call me, Willa," she says. "We haven't heard from him all week."

My hands are shaking as I call Florida.

An older gentleman answers.

JFK's grandfather. "Sorry, dear," he says. "Joseph's gone sailing with Lorna."

Lorna. Sailing with Lorna. JFK loves to sail. After baseball, it's his favorite thing. My mind flashes back to when JFK took me sailing and how I freaked out when I thought the boat would tip. Lorna probably loves to sail.

I picture TaylorSwiftBeyoncé–Lorna in a bikini, zipping across the waves with JFK. Then maybe they'll share a romantic picnic on the beach.

I think of the beach last night with Jess. How sweet it was of him to have held back his feelings for me for more than two years out of respect for his friend. How noble of him. I think of how he looked at me and smiled when he caught my eyes on the dance floor. How quiet he is but yet he opened up to me last night and shared some personal things about his family as he walked me home. How his parents are having problems. He's afraid they're getting divorced. We talked and talked all the way up the porch steps of the inn. "I had a great time, Willa," he said. "Thanks. I mean it, thanks."

Oh, my gosh, I feel like I'm going to explode. My heart is like a washing machine, a jumble of feelings swishing, flipping, tumbling together round and round in the suds. I walk back up to my room. I get out my journal and I write and write, draining out the washing machine . . . slowly beginning to feel better as I do. Thank goodness for my journal. I don't know what I'd do without it.

My phone beeps. A new text. *JFK?*

No. *Jess.*

He says the lady from Poppy Market called. Tonight's band canceled on her. He and Luke are playing again.

"Come, k?" he writes.

I drop down on my bed, stare up at the ceiling, the washing machine revving up again. Joey . . . Jess . . . Joey . . . Jess . . .

Is it possible I like them both?

What should I do?

Who can I talk to?

Mariel? I wish, but I have no way to reach her and I'm not sure she'd understand.

Tina? No. We clicked last night, but what if she slips and tells Ruby and then the whole town will know?

Rosie? No. She's got too much on her mind.

My mother? No way. Besides, she's too wrapped up with the reception.

Sam? No.

Salty barks at me, raising his chin at the end for emphasis.

Will. Good idea. He likes teasing me, but I think if he sees how mixed-up and upset I am he'll do the big-brotherly thing. Maybe he hasn't left for Tina's yet.

I go to look for him. He's not inside. I search the grounds, no Will.

Coming back in through the hallway, the phone rings.

It's Will's friend Chauncey from Martha's Vineyard. He says it's "urgent" he speak with Will.

"I'm trying to find him myself," I say. "Is everything all right?"

"Will's grandmother called here. His grandfather is seriously ill. They need him back home immediately."

Off I run to Tina's house with Salty behind me.

Hopefully, Will is there.

CHAPTER 18

Keep It Simple, Please

♥ ♥ ♥

A word is worth a thousand pictures.
— Elie Wiesel

Tina and Will are sitting side by side in Tina's kitchen eating cupcakes when I find them and tell Will the news.

"Oh, no, Will," Tina says. "I'm sorry."

Will doesn't say anything. He takes another bite of cupcake, then a long drink of milk. He flicks a crumb across the table. He looks up at the photo board hanging on the wall, overflowing with pictures of Tina and her family.

"Could they fit another pretty picture of you up there?" Will says, smiling at Tina.

"Yeah, they really love me," Tina says.

"What's not to love?" Will says.

Tina looks like she's going to cry.

I look around the beautiful gourmet kitchen. I used to be here all the time.

"When do you have to leave?" Tina says to Will. "Maybe my dad will buy me a ticket to London. Maybe I can come with you?"

"Oh, no," Will says, "I wouldn't subject you to the gargoyles. They might eat you alive or dump you in the moat."

We laugh and then everyone is silent again.

Will looks at me and tilts his head.

My heart clenches. He looks younger, scared, like he needs me to be the big sister here. "Come on, Will. We should get home."

"Home?" he repeats, staring at me sadly.

Tina puts her arm around his shoulder.

I know what Will's thinking. How maybe the inn and this town, Bramble, are beginning to really feel like "home" for him. . . . He's got me and Mom and Sam and a pretty girl who's crazy about him, and now he needs to head back across the pond to a cold castle that feels like a morgue and anything but a "home."

"I'll meet you outside," Will says to me.

When he joins me out front, I see his face is wet with tears.

Oh, wow, I guess he and Tina really are falling in love.

When we get back to the Bramblebriar, Will says he needs some time to think. He goes to his room and slams the door.

I hurry to find Sam and tell him what's going on.

"Oh, poor kid," Sam says. "I'll talk to him."

Sam goes to Will's room and knocks. Will lets him in. Sam closes the door. I want to go in, too, but I think Will needs a father's advice right now.

That's what Will needs . . . a father.

Later, Sam comes to see me.

"Will's flying home to London tomorrow evening," he says.

♥ ♥ ♥

Will is not in his room, the porch, the game room, the kitchen.

Finally I find him in the library with Salty Dog.

Will is lying on a couch. Salty is sprawled out on top of him, his face right up close to Will's. They look like they are having a conversation both can understand, which, of course, they are.

When Will sees me, he smiles. "I'm giving Salty instructions for smooth sailing here in America," he says.

A sob slips from my throat. "But he's yours. . . ."

"He's *ours*," Will says.

I start crying.

"Don't worry," Will says. "I'll be back."

"When?" I say.

"Don't know for sure," Will says. "All depends on the gargoyle's condition."

I stifle a laugh. "You really shouldn't call them gargoyles."

"It's the perfect name for them," Will says. "Ancient . . . stone-cold . . . uglier than . . ."

"Your grandparents are ugly?" I say. "How can that be? Look how handsome you are."

"I get my looks from my father's side of the family," Will says. "I get my looks from our dad."

I put on a light jacket and go out for a walk. I head toward Main Street, feeling so bad for Will, and then soon worries for Will turn to worries over JFK and Jess and then back to Will again. I'm not doing too well with that Willa the Warrior thing.

Mrs. Saperstone and Dr. Swammy are coming out of the Quarter Deck restaurant.

"Willa, hello!" Mrs. Saperstone says. "We were just talking about you."

"Yes," Dr. Swammy says. "Thank you for agreeing to plan our wedding."

"My pleasure," I say. "I've been compiling some ideas."

"We want a small and private affair," Mrs. S. says. "Just a very few close friends. Your family, of course. Ms. Toomajian and her husband. A few teachers from Bramble Academy. A few special friends of the library. No more than twenty, I imagine. We are going to ask Mum to do the service at BUC and we want to have the reception in the library garden."

"The library garden?" I say. "But how will we fit tables for dinner and what about a dance floor?"

"We need to . . . *we want to* . . . keep it simple, Willa," Mrs. Saperstone says. "We're thinking just a light buffet, a champagne toast, and cake."

I remember our earlier conversation about finances. "That's fine," I say. "I understand. In fact, I applaud your decision."

Dr. Swammy smiles and nods. "Well, good, then."

"Do you have a date in mind?" I say.

"Well, we have to check with Mum tomorrow, of course," Mrs. S. says. "But if it's okay with her, we'll be married next Saturday. That is, if you're free then, Willa."

"*Next Saturday.* Wow, that's short notice. But I did plan my aunt Ruthie's wedding in the blink of an eye."

"All right, then?" Dr. Swammy says.

"Yes! Don't worry. I won't disappoint you. I promise."

"You could not possibly disappoint us," Mrs. S. says. "Just remember to please keep it simple, okay?"

Out of the corner of my eye I see Ruby Sivler crossing the street. She doesn't look where she's going. . . . A car screeches its brakes to avoid hitting her. "Ruby!" I shout, running toward her.

Ruby looks at me as if she is in a daze. There are black streams of mascara running down her face.

"Oh, Willa," she says. "It's awful."

CHAPTER 19

Ruby's Scary News

♥ ♥ ♥

Fantasy is escapist, and that is its glory. . . . If we value
the freedom of mind and soul, if we're partisans of liberty,
then it's our plain duty to escape, and to take as many
people with us as we can!
— J.R.R. Tolkien

"Ruby . . . what's wrong?" I take her arm and pull her out of harm's way, up onto the sidewalk. There's a bench close by. "Come on, let's sit down."

"I'm so scared, Willa," she says, sobbing, her body shaking like she's freezing.

"About what?" I ask. I touch her hand. I scrounge in my purse for a tissue.

She wipes her face. She shakes her head back and forth.

"What, Ruby?" I say. "You can tell me."

"It's my mom," she says, her face contorting with tears. "She has breast cancer. We found out today."

"Oh, Ruby. I'm sorry." I rub her arm.

"It's bad," Ruby says. "It's already spread. I heard

my father telling my grandmother that it may be too late for . . . for . . . *anything.*" She lets out a horrible sob. I pull her toward me and hug her.

"Oh, Ruby." I rub her back. "It's okay . . . it's okay." I let her cry. I want to say, *I'm sure it's not too late. There are wonderful doctors. Your parents are rich; they'll get the best treatment. Your mom will be fine.* But how can I say that? I don't know if that's true. And so I just hug her and let her cry and rub her back.

"*Willa, what if she dies?*" Ruby shrieks. Some tourists passing by stop and look.

"Ruby. Listen to me." I take her face between my hands, looking straight in her eyes. "With faith all things are possible." This is what Mum and Nana would say. "You've got to be strong for your mom. She'll need you."

"I know," Ruby says. "You're right. It's just so . . . *scary.*"

"Of course it is, honey," I say.

"And I can't find Tina anywhere," Ruby says. "Her phone's off. . . ."

I fill Ruby in on how Will is leaving in the morning. "They are probably wanting to spend every minute of their last night together," I say. "But I'm here."

Ruby sniffles, blows her nose. "Thanks, Willa."

I hand her another tissue.

"Thanks for letting me talk," she says.

"Any time," I say, and I mean it.

"I should be getting back home," Ruby says.

"I'll walk you," I say.

"So what's this I hear about you and Jess?" Ruby says, glad to change the subject.

"What do you mean?" I say.

"Carli told me you and Jess were staring at each other during the concert and she thinks maybe you two went out after since you didn't join us on the beach."

"I went home sick," I say, and then I feel bad for lying, especially as Ruby is being so open with me. This is the most sincere conversation we have ever had.

"Willa," Ruby says. "Listen . . . my mother doesn't want anyone to know about the cancer. She's in total denial right now. It's like if no one else finds out, then it won't really be happening. Do you know what I mean?"

"I hear you," I say. "Don't worry, Rube. I won't say a word."

"Thanks, Willa," Ruby says, leaning over to hug me. "I know we've had our problems, but I think you're great."

"Thanks, Ruby."

Reason: Throw her an olive branch, Willa. Ruby just shared something major with you. Tell her about Jess and JFK.

Willa: No way!

Reason: People can change, Willa. Especially when we give them a chance.

Willa: But she'll tell everyone.

Reason: Are you going to keep Ruby's secret?

Willa: Yes.

Reason: Well, then, why not trust her to do the same?

Letting Reason rule, I tell Ruby about my liking-two-boys-at-once dilemma.

She is surprisingly calm and nice.

"Don't make any rash moves or decisions," she advises. "I've often liked two, three, even four boys at the same time. Trust me, these things have a way of working themselves out in time. In the meantime, just have fun."

I listen. Ruby makes sense.

"Promise me you won't tell anyone," I say.

"Okay," she says.

"Really, Rube, promise."

She promises me she will.

In this moment I think that maybe, just maybe, when Mariel gets back from New York City, all four of us, Tina, Ruby, me, and Mare could all be friends together.

I walk Ruby to her front door.

"Good luck with your mom," I say. "I'll keep her in my prayers. Let me know when you hear anything. And if you want to talk, just call me. Really, Rube, any time."

"I will," Ruby says. "Thanks, Willa."

I turn to leave.

"Hey, Willa," Ruby says.

"Yes?"

"Love the sneakers."

Back at the inn, I look for Will.

"He's out with Tina," Sam says.

I head up to my room and write in my journal. I plop down on my bed, check my messages. Still no response from JFK. The song was beautiful, such a nice gift, but why is he ignoring me?

I tear open some saltwater taffies and start reading *Firegirl*. The beginning reminds me of *Stargirl* by Jerry Spinelli, one of my favorite books.

Here in *Firegirl*, the girl's name is Jessica. The *Jess* in Jessica jumps out at me and my mind wanders.

I never let Jessie know I wasn't coming to his concert tonight.

I wonder why?

CHAPTER 20

Open to the Opportunities

♥ ♥ ♥

*I have sometimes dreamt that when the Day of Judgment
dawns . . . the Almighty will turn to Peter . . . when He sees
us coming with our books under our arms, and say "Look,
these need no reward. We have nothing to give them here.
They have loved reading."*

— Virginia Woolf

Early Sunday morning, there is a knock on my door.

"Want to join me for a run before church?" my
mother says.

"Sure, Mom. I'll be right down." I look at the clock.
I hurry and get dressed.

Out in the hallway I pause by Captain Ahab. My
brother Will's room. Come tonight, he will be gone.
Who knows if and when he'll ever come back.

Mom drives us into Falmouth. I listen as she shares
all the highlights of the Bennigan reception and how
absolutely thrilled the bride's family was and the wedding party, too, and how three of the bridesmaids said
they expect to be engaged by summer's end and "they

want a wedding just like Star Bennigan's here at the Bramblebriar."

"Will they be braviars?" I say.

"Absolutely," Mom says, "probably worse than Ms. Star. They'll probably want original one-of-a-kind dinner entrees, not just desserts, and I'll be happy to charge them accordingly."

"That's great, Mom," I say, laughing. "Good for you."

"No, good for *business*," she says.

We park near the Shining Sea pathway.

"Do you think you can do three and a half out and three and a half back?" Mom says.

"Seven miles," I say. "I'm not sure."

"Do what you can, then," she says. "You need to start extending your distance if you're going to run the Falmouth Road Race with me next month."

"Okay, Mom, I'll try."

We stretch, check our watches, and we're off.

It's still cool, a beautiful morning, perfect for a run.

The path takes us through a wooded area, then out along the ocean. It's nice huffing and puffing beside my mother, my heart pumping fast. I know Mom's purposely keeping her pace down so we can stay together. She's in awesome shape.

I look at my mother, so young-looking, healthy, and

beautiful — that jet-black hair with no grays yet, those stunning green eyes, alabaster cheeks, her skin so pale despite our living by the ocean. My mom is religious about wearing sunblock and hats to protect her skin from the sun.

I think about Mrs. Sivler, Ruby's mother, about how when I saw her the other day, I rolled my eyes, thinking how she was dressed like a teenager. How foolish she was pining over that poodle like it was a person. Now I feel bad for her. How frightened she must be. I wish I could tell my mother about the cancer diagnosis, but I did give my promise to Ruby.

Back home, I go to the kitchen to grab a muffin. Rosie is putting a tray of quiche in the oven. Her last day. She leaves tonight.

"Tell Sulamina Mum I said hello," Rosie says. "Tell her my good news."

"Oh, I will," I say. "She'll be so happy for you, Rosie."

Running upstairs to my room, I can barely contain my excitement as I shower and get dressed for church. I put on a white top, a pink skirt, and my new pink sneakers. *Mum, Mum . . . Mum, Mum, Mum*, plays the melody in my head. I cannot wait to see her!

At a quarter to eleven, Sam, Mom, Will, and I set

off toward Nana's to pick her up so we can all walk to BUC together.

"Guess what," Nana says. "That sweet Mr. Taylor had such a nice experience at our store that he said he's going to encourage his friend Sheryl to do a signing here when her new book comes out next month."

"Sheryl who?" I say.

"Sheryl Crow," Nana says.

"*Sheryl Crow!?*" my mother shrieks. "Oh, my gosh, I love her."

"Me, too," Sam says with a sly grin.

"Watch it, buster," my mother says, playfully elbowing Sam's arm.

When we reach town and BUC is in sight, I cannot wait a second longer.

"See you there," I say, and off I go, running all the way — down the street, up the stairs, across the lobby. There she is!

"Mum!" I shout.

"Willa!"

I race to her and she swoops me up, her billowy rainbow-striped vestment swirling out around us as she hug-dances me about.

"How's my favorite girl in the whole world?" Mum says.

"I couldn't be happier, Mum," I say. "Now that you're back."

Mum's big brown eyes, her warm, warm smile, her beautiful face is shining just as I remembered it. She looks thinner, though, much thinner actually.

"What about me, little mama?" Riley, Mum's husband, says. "Where's my sugar this morning?"

"Hi, Riley!" I laugh. Riley hugs me. I kiss his cheek.

"Look how pretty you are, all grown up," he says. "What are you, in college now? We sure did miss you, sugar."

"Missed you more," I say.

Inside, the congregation is positively bee-buzzing with joy at having Sulamina Mum back with us. The pews are packed, everyone bubbling with happy conversation.

Mum's nephew, Rob, sits with us. "Where've you been, stranger?" I ask him.

"Trying to dodge the authors," he says, jokingly referring to Tina and Ruby.

The Belles, Tina's family, sit down a few rows behind us, and when Tina and Will lock eyes, Tina looks like she's going to burst into tears.

Will whispers something to Sam and then makes his way out of our pew to go back and sit with Tina.

I feel bad for the two of them. They just really connected and now Will is leaving.

Will is leaving. My heart hurts.

Over there is JFK's family, Mr. and Mrs. Kennelly and JFK's little brother, Brendan. I feel a punch in my stomach. Brendan waves at me and I wave back. I think of JFK. I think of Jess. When I turn back around in my seat, my mother is looking at me. "Everything okay?" she says.

Mrs. Saperstone and Dr. Swammy come in and take a seat. They smile and nod at me. The "S.'s" I'll call them from now on. I need to finish planning their wedding pronto — later today after Rosie leaves, after Will leaves, when I stop crying long enough to put on my happy face again and can focus on their special day.

The organist starts playing and we stand to sing *" 'Tis a gift to be simple, 'tis a gift to be free . . ."*

I hear a shuffle and out of the corner of my eye I see the Sivlers, Ruby and her mom and dad, and older sister home from college. Mrs. Sivler is dressed in a tailored turquoise linen pantsuit with matching turquoise and silver jewelry, her red hair swept back off her shoulders. Her face, usually garishly made up, has a lot less makeup this morning. She is eerily expressionless.

Then, as if Mrs. Sivler knows she's being watched and wants to keep up appearances, a smile crosses her face and she raises her chin up.

Mum takes the pulpit, and as I knew she would, she wastes no time calling on each of us to think about our lives, how we are *using* our lives.

"Don't just drop off three cans of soup at a food pantry or write a check and be done," she says. "Every day, each and every day, be open to the opportunities to serve that will arise. Be ready and waiting to serve."

I think about how I can't wait to make CHANGE FOR GOOD ✪ jugs for Mum and Riley. And wait till Mum hears about my plan to give all my books away!

In an hour, the service is over. "In conclusion," Mum says, "the great and talented funny lady Erma Bombeck once said, 'When I stand before God at the end of my life, I would hope that I would not have a single bit of talent left, and could say, "I used everything you gave me."' That, my friends, is my challenge to you this day. Go and use everything God has given you. Do not waste a precious moment. Go, go, go, go, go, go. Go!"

My eyes are drawn back to Mrs. Sivler. Her head is resting on Mr. Sivler's shoulder. Ruby is rubbing her mother's arm. A cry catches in my throat.

As the congregation files out, I see Jessie with his mother, and my heart skips a beat. I didn't know they were here! I'm not watching where I'm going and I plunge into Mr. Wickstrom. "Oh, I'm sorry," I say. I look back over to where Jess was standing, but now he's gone. My mother is observing all of this. She looks at me and squints her eyes like *Hmmmm . . . What have we here?*

I move ahead and out into the lobby area. Mrs. Saperstone and Dr. Swammy are talking with Mum. Mum makes a whooping sound, claps her hands in the air, and dances around a bit. Clearly they have shared their happy news with her.

Good, now the wedding planner can proceed with the reception.

"What time will the service be?" I ask Dr. Swammy.

"Five P.M. Saturday," he says.

Mrs. Saperstone nods. "And the reception right after at six in the library garden. Okay, Willa?"

"Sounds good," I say. "I'll have a plan to show you tomorrow."

"Good," Mrs. S. says. "We'll start calling our friends."

The Sivlers are waiting next to speak with Mum. Mr. Sivler talks and I see Mum nodding her head solemnly. When he's done, Mum takes Mrs. Sivler in her arms and hugs her. They hug for a long time. Then Mum thrusts her fist up in the air in what looks like a fighting stance. She pushes that fist up, up, up in the air.

Good, I'm glad Mrs. Sivler shared her secret. Mum will help her get through this for sure.

Riley is standing in the corner, sipping coffee. I go over to talk with him.

I tell him how Mrs. Saperstone and Dr. Swammy are getting married next Saturday and how I am planning their wedding reception. "So that's what they were talking to Sully about just now," he says. "Sully" is Riley's special name for Mum. "Sully sure looked happy for them. . . . I wonder what those other people, with the lady in the blue suit, were talking to Sully about. Did you see her pushing her fist up, all powerful?"

I hesitate, but since clearly the Sivlers confided in Mum, and Mum surely will discuss this with Riley, I tell him about Mrs. Sivler having breast cancer.

Riley sets down his coffee. He looks at me with a confusing expression.

"What?" I say.

"That's one of the reasons we came back here," Riley says.

"What's that?" I say.

"I'm sure Mum is planning to tell you herself. She wanted everything to be happy this morning, her first day back, but . . ."

I get this awful feeling. "But what, Riley. *What?*"

And even before he says it, I know.

"Mum has breast cancer, too, Willa."

My body goes cold.

"She'll be starting treatment next week."

CHAPTER 21

One Hello, Two Good-byes

♥ ♥ ♥

Often I sat up in my room reading the greatest part of the night, when the book was borrowed in the evening and to be returned early in the morning, lest it should be missed or wanted.

— Benjamin Franklin

Mum has cancer? I am frozen solid with the shock of this.

No, it can't be. Not Mum. Just when she and Riley finally found each other and got married? Just when she's come home here to Bramble?

No, this just isn't right. It's just not fair. Do you hear me, God?

Do you hear me?

I picture Mum with Mrs. Sivler at church. Mum listening to Sherry Sivler so empathetically, then pumping her fist up in the air and getting Mrs. Sivler to do the same.

Reason: That's the right attitude. Be strong and fight.

Willa: I know, but it's Mum, *Mum*. . . .

Reason: And what did you say to Ruby? You told her to be strong for her mother.

Willa: I know, but it's Mum. . . . *Mum* . . .

Reason: You said with faith all things are possible. Who taught you that?

Willa: Mum.

Reason: Well, then?

Willa: I will be strong and have faith and believe for Mum.

Reason: That's the spirit.

♥   ♥   ♥

When we get home from BUC, Will says he's off to see Tina. He'll be back soon. I wish he would spend this last afternoon with me, but I understand it's a matter of the heart.

Reason: Really, Willa? You understand about heart matters?

Willa: No, Reason. I don't. Don't act so smug.

I think about Joey. I think about Jess.

I think I am horribly, hopelessly confused.

I think there's nothing I can do at the moment.

I go to the kitchen. Rosie has Lilly with her.

"Hey, little girl," I say, bending down to pick up Lilly.

"Will-wa," she says, laughing. She kisses my cheek. She points to my eye and then pokes it.

"Ouch," I say, "that hurt."

"Lilly!" Rosie admonishes her daughter.

Lilly giggles.

"Sorry, Willa," Rosie says. "She's got this fascination with eyes lately."

"That's okay." I look at Lilly. "That hurt, Lilly. Boo-boo."

Lilly gets it. She looks remorseful.

"It's okay, Lilly. I love you."

Lilly hugs me. I hug her back.

"When are you going, Rosie?"

"Right after lunch," she says.

"Don't leave until I get back," I say, rushing out the door.

"As if!" Rosie shouts behind me. "Crazy girl."

I bike fast to Sweet Bramble Books. Nana and Dr. Swammy are off today. Two of Nana's best workers, Kristen and Amy, back home on Cape for the summer, are managing the store.

"How's college going?" I ask.

Kristen is an English/Education major at Le Moyne in upstate New York. Amy is studying Health Care Administration at the University of Rhode Island.

They fill me in on the highlights.

"Won't be long and you'll be starting to look at schools, Willa," Kristen says. "You'll be a sophomore this year, right?"

"She's got time," Amy says. "Junior year's when you really start the process, but make sure you keep your grades up and participate in lots of clubs and sports and things."

"And community service," Kristen adds. "Colleges are really big on that."

"I'm really big on that, too," I say. I tell them about my From Cape Cod, With Love plan to leave free books in public places that will hopefully be passed on and on.

"Great idea," Kristen says.

"Love it," Amy agrees.

In the young children's section, I find the board book versions of *Goodnight Moon* and *The Very Hungry Caterpillar.* In the cooking section, I buy the nice hardcover copy of *From Julia Child's Kitchen.* In the YA fiction section, I see a display with author David Almond's latest release. I have Amy check. The book just came out this month. Chances are good Will doesn't have it yet. He's been so focused on his wild goose chase to find our birthfather, long since deceased, and now, more recently, on Tina.

I write messages inside the books for Rosie and Will. Amy rings up my purchases and Kristen wraps them.

Outside, I pass by the dollar store. That reminds me. I head inside.

A clerk shows me the aisle where the blank books are.

They have quite a nice selection.

I buy enough for each of the guest rooms in the main house and a bag of pens so we can get started on the journal idea Mom and Sam agreed to.

Back at Bramblebriar, I go to the kitchen to give Rosie and Lilly their going-away-good-luck presents.

Lilly giggles at the covers and pokes the caterpillar's eye.

Inside Rosie's cookbook I had written:

Someday you'll be as famous as Julia.
The whole world will love Sweet Rosie's Sweets.
Your friend always,
Willa

Rosie cries when she reads this inscription. "I love you, Willa," she says.

"Love you, too, Rosie. Always."

♥ ♥ ♥

Rosie's friend Tara comes to pick up Rosie and Lilly.

Rosie hugs Sam and they say good-bye.

Rosie hugs Mom and my mother hands her an envelope.

When Rosie opens it, she gasps. "But you paid me already, Stella," Rosie says, shaking her head. She hands the envelope back to my mother.

"No, Rosie. This is your bonus," my mother says, refusing the envelope. "You deserve it. The Bennigan wedding was a hit because of your one hundred cakes.

Sam and I insist that you take this gift with our gratitude and best wishes."

Sam puts his arm around my mother.

I love my mother. The Braviar Queen. She's got a big heart after all.

Rosie wipes away tears. So do I.

"Till soon, Willa," she says.

"Till soon, Rosie." I kiss her good-bye.

Lilly's chewing on the corner of one of her new books.

"Hey, don't eat the caterpillar," I say, and we laugh.

Lilly points her finger at the caterpillar's eye and says something. She turns the page and says something else.

"Good reading, Lilly!" I say. "Good reading."

After Rosie and Lilly leave, I head up to Will's room.

The door is slightly ajar. I enter. He's not there. His bags are packed. He's made the bed — the sloppy way boys do, but at least he tried.

"Spyin' on me, are ya?" Will says, entering the room, making his voice sound like a pirate.

"I wish you didn't have to go," I say, smoothing the quilt on his bed.

"I wish I didn't, either," he says.

"Will you come back?" I say.

And then Mom and Sam are there in the doorway. They look sad but are trying to be cheerful for Will's sake and mine.

"We need to get moving, Will, if we're going to get you to Logan Airport on time," Sam says.

Mom hands Will some bills. "Money for dinner," she says.

"Thanks, Stella," Will says, "but I'm all set. One thing the gargoyles are good at giving is money."

"The gargoyles?" Stella says.

Will and I laugh.

"Private joke," I say.

"Willa, here," Will says. He hands me a Bramblebriar coffee mug filled with change. "For that jug you've got," he says.

"Thanks," I say. "And this is for you."

He unwraps the present. "Thanks!" he says. "Something to read on the plane." He opens the cover, reads the FROM THE LIBRARY OF label.

"From Cape Cod, With Love, huh?" he says.

"Yes," I say. "When you're done reading it, leave it in a public place back in London, some place where someone can pick it up and read it and pass it along. . . ."

"What a sweet idea," my mother says. "But that's a hardcover book. Are you sure you want to do that?"

Will looks at me. I nod at him.

"Oh, yes," he says, "we're sure. Right, little sister?"

At the word *sister*, I can't hold the tears back any longer.

He hugs me. "There, there."

I don't want to let him go. "Are you coming back?" I whisper in his ear.

"Yes," Will says. "I promise."

"Promise?" I repeat.

"Promise."

I walk Will out to Sam's car.

"I told Tina the duke's daughter thing was a fib," Will says. "Couldn't have her worrying about that while I'm away."

Oh, good, that's right. Tina. Yet another reason for my brother to come back.

"Bye! Bye! Safe trip!" Mom and I say as Sam and Will drive off.

I go to my room and lie on my bed. What an unbelievable Sunday.

One hello, two good-byes.

My cell phone beeps.

I check my messages.

Two from Joey, three from Jess.

Does that mean Jess likes me more?

CHAPTER 22

Heart-to-Heart

♥ ♥ ♥

My alma mater was books, a good library. . . . I could
spend the rest of my life reading, just satisfying my
curiosity.

    — Malcolm X

Sunday night, five o'clock. I must have dozed off.
I wonder what we're doing for dinner? Sitting at
my desk, I open my journal, *From the Life of Willa*
Havisham, and begin to write about all that has been
happening this past week . . . how in just one week of
my life, it's as if I've lived a whole year. Rosie going,
Mum coming, Will going, Jess here, JFK gone; The S.'s
getting engaged, such happy news; Mrs. Sivler and Mum
both being diagnosed with cancer, such scary news . . .

My mother knocks and asks if she can come in.

"Sure, Mom." I close my journal and slide it into a
drawer.

"Sam back from the airport yet?" I say.

"No, but he should be here any moment."

My mother sits on my bed. "I have some news to share with you," she says, and by the tone of her voice I can tell it's not happy.

More bad news? I don't think I can take one single ounce more. I wonder if perhaps she and Sam had another miscarriage. I thought they had decided not to try and have another baby, but were going to adopt. . . .

"Ruby's mother has breast cancer," Mom says.

"Yes, I know. Ruby told me."

"Oh, I see," she says, looking relieved. "And do you also know that Mum . . ."

"Yes," I say. "Riley told me this morning."

"Nana shared the news with me," my mother says. She lets out a long, sad sigh, shaking her head back and forth. "It's just not right."

"My sentiments exactly," I say.

"I called both Mum and Sherry just now," my mother says, "to let them know we are here for them, to drive to treatments, to run errands, cook, shop, whatever."

"That's good of you, Mom."

"That's what friends do," my mother says. "As soon as I find out their radiation or chemotherapy schedules,

Sam and I will help with driving and we'll see that dinners are delivered to their houses during the weeks they are receiving treatments so that neither Mum nor Sherry will have to concern themselves with that."

"I told Ruby that I was here for her and to call me any time."

"Don't wait for a call, Willa," my mother says. "Make sure that you and Tina and the other girls check in on Ruby regularly and let her talk when she needs to, and plan some cheerful outings to take her mind off her worries."

"Good idea, Mom. I'll call Tina and everybody."

My mother looks around my room. She clears her throat. She turns to me. "Okay, now," she says, locking my eyes in hers. "How about *you*? How's my daughter doing?"

"Okay," I say, a bit unsettled. It's seldom that my mother and I ever have a heart-to-heart. She's always so busy. At least we do have running together.

"I'm so sad that Will had to go."

"I know," Mom says. "Me, too. Such a fine young man."

"I was hoping you and Sam might adopt him."

"*Adopt him?*" Mother says. "But he has family in England, Willa."

"His grandparents are horrible," I say. "They live in a castle with tons of servants, but they didn't know what to do with a teenage boy, so they shipped him off to boarding school and —"

"Are the grandparents the gargoyles you and Will were talking about?"

"Yes!" I say.

Mom laughs. "Gargoyles. That's funny."

"It's not funny for Will," I say.

"No," she says. "I'm sure it isn't. I feel so bad for the boy. No mother. No father. But at least now he has a sister." She smiles and brushes a loose strand of hair off of my forehead. "And a wonderful sister at that. I'm sure you'll see him again soon. Maybe we can even plan for a trip to London."

Mom smiles as she looks around my room. Her gaze rests on my dresser. She nods at the CHANGE FOR GOOD ✪ jug. "You should see mine," she says. "It's filling up quickly. That was a great idea you had."

"Thanks, Mom."

"Oh, and," she says, "Darryl showed me the journal that was in Mrs. Noonan's room. She wrote such lovely things about the inn. So did Mr. Halloran. That was another great idea."

I tell my mother more about my latest idea . . . about sending my books out into the world . . . free . . . and hopefully starting a chain reaction. . . . Who knows how far they will spread.

My mother's lips quiver and she looks like she's going to cry. "You never cease to amaze me, Willa. Truly. I am so very proud of you."

"Oh, and guess what," I say. "Happy news! Mrs. Saperstone and Dr. Swaminathan are engaged and they've asked me to plan their wedding."

"Really? Wow. When are they getting married?"

"Next Saturday."

"Next Saturday!" my mother shouts. "Obviously they aren't expecting to have their wedding here at the inn."

"No, Mom," I say. "They want a very modest, very simple affair."

"Oh," Mom says, sounding disappointed. "Like what?"

"Mum will do the service at BUC, of course, and then I am planning their reception in the garden behind the library."

Mom raises her eyebrows. "What about dinner and a band and . . ."

"I'll figure it all out," I say. "Mrs. S. and Dr. Swammy are going to be calling all of their guests to invite —"

"Calling them?" my mother says, grimacing. "No invitations?"

"No," I say, shrugging my shoulders, no big deal. "They are only inviting twenty or so close friends, and given the short notice, Mrs. S. thought a phone call would be the quickest and most personal way."

"Who'll be catering it?" Mom says.

"I haven't figured that part out exactly yet, but Mrs. S. said she wanted a very simple buffet so I was thinking of asking the restaurants on Main Street to each send a platter of fancy finger foods, something with a literary theme. . . ."

"Finger foods," my mother says. "What . . . no sit-down dinner?"

My mother is getting flustered with all of this.

"Relax, Mom," I say. "I've got it under control."

"But, Willa . . ." Then my mother stops. She smiles at me. She nods. "Okay, then. If you need any help, let me know." She stands up. She looks at me. "Would you allow me to furnish the wedding cake, compliments of the Bramblebriar Inn, as a gift to the bride and groom? Hopefully, the new baker Sam hired will be starting this week."

"Sure, Mom, that's so nice. Thank you."

"And what about a photographer?"

"Mom . . . Mom, stop. I've got this. Are you forgetting that I grew up in the business? That I have more than a decade of experience in the field? That I am the daughter of the hottest wedding planner on the East Coast?"

Mom laughs. "Just the East Coast?"

My phone beeps. I glance down.

It's a new text from Jess. My heart flips.

I think to tell my mother. To let her know how conflicted I am feeling about JFK and Jess . . . to ask for her advice . . .

"Who's the boy?" she says.

"*What?*" I gulp.

"I'm right, aren't I?" my mother says. She smiles at me. "With Joseph Kennelly away, I imagine there are other Bramble boys hoping for a date with my beautiful daughter."

Beautiful daughter? I let that slide.

"Who was that boy at church this morning?" Mom says.

I knew she saw me looking at Jess.

"Isn't he in that band that played at the dances you and your friends had in the barn to raise money for the library?"

"His name is Jess. And yes, he's in the band, the Buoy Boys."

"He's very cute," my mother says.

"Yes," I say.

"And so is Joseph," my mother says.

"Yes," I say. "And it's not just that they're cute. They are both really nice and kindhearted and interesting and fun. . . ."

"And they both like you," my mother says.

"Yes."

"And you like both of them?" she says.

I nod my head.

"Well, what a lovely summer situation," she says.

A lovely summer situation. Did she just say that?

My mother laughs. "This reminds me of the summer Scott Wickstrom and Seth Muhlfelder both had a crush on me. Or was it I had a crush on them? Both, as I recall. Scott and I had been going to the movies together, and then Seth invited me sailing."

"You like to sail?" I say.

"I used to love it," my mother says.

I think about Lorna and JFK sailing.

"So you were dating Scott, but then Seth and you went sailing."

"Yep." My mother shakes her head back and forth, smiling, clearly enjoying this stroll down memory lane.

"And so what did you do?" I say. "How did you decide?"

"I didn't *do* or decide anything," my mother says. "I enjoyed the attention and giggled about it with my girlfriends and by the end of the summer, it was over."

"Well, who did you end up sticking with?" I say. "Scott or Seth?" Scott the boyfriend. Seth the drummer. "Was Seth a drummer?" I ask.

"Gosh, no," my mother says, laughing.

My heart is beating fast. So much rides on my mother's answer. "And so who did you end up with?"

"Neither," my mom says.

"What?"

"Sophomore year started and classes were challenging and there was cheerleading practice. . . ."

"You were a cheerleader?" I say. How did I not know this before?

"Captain," my mother says. "And then a really cute boy on the varsity basketball team, Ryan Butler, who was a junior, caught my eye and by spring I had the courage to ask him to the Sophomore Soiree and he said yes."

"What happened to Scott and Seth?" I say.

My mother shrugs her shoulders and smiles. "They moved on and dated other people, too. That's what you do in high school."

"But that was years ago," I say.

My mother swats my arm playfully. "Hey, come on, Willa. I'm not a dinosaur."

We laugh.

"I know," I say. "But things are different now."

"Really?" my mother says. "Two boys liking the same girl, the same summer? One girl liking two boys at the same time? It's an age-old story, Willa. It's how it's supposed to be. How will you ever know you've found 'the one' if you've only ever dated one boy?"

"That's exactly what Tina said."

"Smart girl," my mom says.

"Yes indeed," Sam says. He's standing in the doorway, beaming at us. "Like mother, like daughter. Smart and beautiful, too."

Mom smiles at Sam and when she does, I see just how very much she loves him.

"Will's flight get off okay?" I say.

"Yes," Sam says. "Great kid. It was nice having him here. A man can sure feel outnumbered in this family of strong women," he says.

"Oh, Sam," my mother says.

"How about we go out to dinner?" I suggest.

"Sounds good," Sam says.

"I'd love some chowder and a lobster roll," Mom says. (My mother refuses to drop the "er" and do the "a'" thing.) "Let's hit the Raw Bar at Poppy Marketplace."

Poppy Marketplace? What if the Buoy Boys are playing again tonight? I start to say, "No, can we go somewhere else," but I can see my mom's got her heart set on that lobsta' roll.

CHAPTER 23

The Moonrise

♥   ♥   ♥

Blessed be the inventor of the alphabet, pen and printing press! Life would be to me in all events a terrible thing without books.
— Lucy Maud Montgomery

When we pull into the parking lot across from Poppy Marketplace, I hear the music playing.

Mom reads the blackboard out front. CONCERT TONITE, THE BUOY BOYS, 7–9 P.M.

Oh, no, just what I was afraid of.

"That's your friend's band, right?" Mom says. She raises her eyebrows and smiles.

I nod. "Come on. Let's go eat."

We make our way along the crushed-shell pathway. A little boy comes toward me with a three-scoop-high ice cream cone covered with rainbow sprinkles. It's so big he can hardly see over it. I move to prevent a collision.

The dance floor is there on the right, crowded with little ducks doing their thing. Luke is singing

"California Girls," and then a dancing mother with a baby in her arms moves, and I see him, Jess, on the drums.

I stop walking. He spots me, too. His eyes widen, surprised. I nod. He nods.

"Let's get a table," Mom says, and we head to Bobby's for dinner.

I order a cup of chowder. Mom and Sam order chowder and lobster rolls.

The courtyard door swings open and who comes in but JFK's parents, the Kennellys. There aren't any free tables left. Mom motions for them to join us. *Oh, no.*

When my chowder comes, I can barely eat it. I put one oyster cracker on top at a time and swirl it around until it's covered with soup.

The adults talk about news in town. Mum being back. Mrs. Kennelly meeting James Taylor. Plans to replenish the sand on the Spit, plans for resurfacing a beach parking lot, the controversy over the wind towers planned for Nantucket Sound. My mind drifts off. I hear Jess and Luke playing "Surfin' Safari."

"How are your boys doing?" Sam asks the Kennellys.

"Poor Joey's just about had it with Florida," Mrs. Kennelly says. "I'm sure you've been hearing that, Willa."

I turn my attention to her, feeling my stomach clench at the sound of Joey's name.

"He's really not getting any baseball experience," Mrs. Kennelly says, "and the heat is killing him, just stifling this time of year. He got a buzz cut, but . . ."

JFK got a buzz cut. Why didn't he tell me that? I try to picture him bald.

The grown-ups order another round of drinks. They'll be here a while. The music has stopped; the Buoys must be taking a break.

"I'm going to go walk around," I say.

I find Jess in the pizza place. "Hey, Willa," he says. My heart feels all fluttery inside. "Hi, Jess."

He's just about to cash out. "Want a slushie?" he says. "They're good."

"Yes, sure, thanks."

He pays for our order and we find a spot to sit atop a picnic table in the mini-golf area. I notice how my knees look next to his.

A group of young girls comes forward within inches of us and stops. They are all dressed up, wearing lots of sparkly stuff. They whisper and giggle and stare at Jess.

"I've got groupies," he says in my ear. "They've been here all three nights."

I laugh. "I see. Listen. . . . I'm sorry I couldn't make it last . . ."

"No worries." Jess shrugs his shoulders. "I was just letting you know. Luke and I lucked out. Some problem with whoever they booked. The crowd likes us. The manager may hire us for the summer. Good thing. I need the cash. I want to buy a car."

"Don't you have to be sixteen to drive?"

"I am sixteen," Jess says.

"Oh."

"You're dating an older guy," he says.

The slushie slushes down my throat. "Am I? Are we . . . *dating*?"

"I'm in," Jess says, locking those gorgeous brown eyes to mine. "What about you?"

"Jess . . . *come on*!" Luke is standing there looking annoyed. "Where the heck have you been? Let's go, second set."

Jess tosses his plate and cup in the trash, stands up. He touches my hand. He looks at me. "Will you stick around?" he says.

"Jess . . . *now*," Luke says. "Come on, dude. Let's not lose this gig."

I am so conflicted, so confused. "I don't know, Jess," I say. "I'm here with my parents and . . ."

"No worries," Jess says, shrugging his shoulders and walking.

"Maybe," I call after him. I need some time to think. I watch until he is out of sight.

One of the groupies is looking up at me with this smarty-pants smirk on her face.

"He's way too old for you," I say.

She tosses her head and runs off to join the other sparklers.

Instead of rejoining my parents, I walk across the street, past the Popponesset Inn, out to the beach. I turn right and head toward a lifeguard chair. I climb up and sit where Ruby sat the other night.

The water is ink blue, white frothy foam waves lapping in against the sand. A few lights twinkle off-shore from distant boats. Way over there, the lighthouse beacon.

I close my eyes, breathe in and out.

What do I do about JFK and Jess?

I think about what my mother said, about what Ruby said, but what do I think? How do I feel? It isn't their life; it's mine. From the moment I first met him, I fell in love with JFK. But yet, I feel something so strong for Jess now. Is it love? What is love? Life was so simple when my two favorite things were books and candy. Now my two favorite things are . . .

A gull squawks. I open my eyes. There before me is an amazing sight. . . . There should be megaphones announcing this, a stadium crown assembled to watch. . . .

The moon, a gigantic golden sugar cookie, is rising up out of the sea right before me.

A moonrise?

Oh, how beautiful.

I have seen the sunrise countless times, but the moonrise . . . never.

Why this moment? Why this night? Is this coincidence or a sign for me?

I think I hear a giggle. Water splashes.

Is this *a mermaid gift*?

Later, at home, in bed, I open *Out of the Dust*. It's written in free verse, sort of like a poem. I think about how JFK loves to write rap lyrics. "It's like poetry, but it's music," he says.

I put on my headphones, listen to my song. How sweet of him to write a song for me and have it recorded. If that's not love, I don't know what is.

No, actually, I don't know what love is.

I have absolutely no idea.

Life was so easy when I was seven or eight . . . the age of those sparkly little "groupies" flirting with Jess tonight . . . scrunchie things in their hair, bags of candy in their hands.

I thought love was supposed to feel wonderful.

No one said how much it would hurt.

CHAPTER 24

Lovebirds and Love Hurts

♥ ♥ ♥

Though reading may not at first blush
seem like an act of creation, in a deep sense it is.
Without the enthusiastic reader, who is really the
author's counterpart and very often his most secret rival;
a book would die.

— Henry Miller

On Monday I'm not scheduled to work. I get up early and sit at my desk, sketching out plans for the S.'s wedding reception on Saturday. I need to check the lighting in the library garden. I'll ask Sam to help me string twinkle lights among the trees. Mom will certainly let me borrow a few folding banquet tables for the buffet, and tablecloths and linens, dishes and glasses, too.

I head into town and speak with the owners of the restaurants Mrs. S. and Dr. S. are patrons of. It's a bit too complicated to come up with hors d'oeuvres with a literary theme on such short notice, but each kindly agrees to supply a platter of appetizers for "A Taste of Bramble's Best" in honor of the bride and groom. I promise to make little name cards saying which restaurant each dish is from. Mom already said she'd take care of the cake. I'll borrow a punch bowl and cups from the inn. There's a nice punch recipe in the file in the kitchen. As for the champagne toast . . . I'll have to ask Sam and Mom how much champagne to buy for twenty guests. I'll ask the S.'s what kind of music they'd like played and maybe Jess will help me put together a few sets and Mom will let me borrow her new iPod party thing. . . . Decorations? The garden is in bloom. The whale spoutin' fountain is so pretty. I know. . . . I'll bring pennies . . . give one to each guest and ask each to share a "wish" for the newlyweds and then toss the coin into the fountain. That will be a unique and original twist just for the S.'s wedding. . . .

I look over my notes and make my To-Do list.

♥   ♥   ♥

Outside, I bike straight to Mum's.
She's so happy to see me. "Come in, come in!"
She makes us tea. We sit at her kitchen table.
"How are you doing?" I ask.

I don't mention the cancer, but Mum knows what I mean.

"I'm fine, little sister, I'm fine. I've got a good doctor. She says they found it early. I start radiation a week from today."

"What can I do to help?" I ask.

"Use your life to make a difference," Mum says, "and say 'thank you' every day."

We laugh.

"I know, Mum. I got it. But what can I do for *you*?"

"You can check in on my man if they decide to keep me in the hospital for any reason. He's trying to act all big and strong, but I know he's scared."

"Sure, Mum. I'll come visit Riley. We'll have him over to the inn for dinner and I'll whup his butt at chess or bocce or croquet."

"You're not going to make me exercise, are you?" Riley says, coming into the kitchen.

"Morning, Mama," he says to Mum, bending down to kiss his wife.

"Morning, sugar," he says to me, tapping my cheek.

"Darn right she is," Mum says. "Gotta make sure you're as healthy as can be. You've got some years on me, old man. I want to make sure you'll be rocking next to me on that porch out there when our rocking chair days come."

Riley stands and pulls Mum up out of her chair. "Baby, we're a long way from rocking chair days." He takes Mum's hand, wraps his arms around her body, and they start dancing, real slow and sexy like.

"Hmm . . . hmmm . . . it's getting hot in this kitchen this morning," Mum says.

"You cooking something, Mama?" Riley says.

They laugh.

"See you two lovebirds later!" I say.

♥　　♥　　♥

Back home, there's a text from JFK to call him at his grandparents'.

I find his grandparents' number. I am so nervous. *What if someone saw me and Jess together at the beach Friday or saw us at Poppy Marketplace last night?*

JFK answers. "I miss you!" he says.

"I miss you, too," I say.

"What's up?" he says.

I tell him about Will having to go back to England.

"Bon voyage," JFK says sarcastically. He didn't like Will, didn't trust him.

"You misjudged him, Joey," I say. "Will is actually really nice."

I tell him about Ruby's mom and Mum both having breast cancer.

"That sucks," he says.

"I know," I say. "I hope they'll be okay."

"Did you go to the concert the other night?" JFK says.

He says it fast. It takes me a second to realize he really said it.

My heart starts drumming, boom, boom, boom.

"Yeah . . . no . . . well, just for a little while, but then I felt sick and went home."

There is complete silence. Silence, silence, silence.

"Are you there, Joey?"

"Yeah, I'm here."

There is a strange edge to his voice. Is it anger?

"Yeah, I'm here. In Florida. Thousands of miles away. And my girlfriend and a guy who I thought was my friend . . ."

"Wait, Joey."

"Wait nothing, Willa. I thought we were tight. I thought you loved me."

"I do, Joey, I do."

Click.

He hung up on me. I redial the number. An answering machine picks up. I redial. The machine picks up again.

How did he find out? Who would have called him to tell him?

And then I know.

Ruby. It had to have been.

I sit. I feel physically sick inside.

What have I done? Have I lost JFK for good?

I rush to get the locket. I put it on. I open the two halves of the heart. I close them so Joey and I are kissing.

I collapse on my bed. I cry and cry. Oh, my gosh, this hurts.

I hate you, Ruby. I hate you, Ruby.

Reason: You have no proof it was her, Willa.

Willa: Shut up, Reason. I hate you, too.

CHAPTER 25

A Perfect Wedding

♥　♥　♥

The books I read are the ones I knew and loved when I was a young man and to which I return as you do to friends. . . . I've read these books so often that I don't always begin at page one and read on to the end. I just read one scene, or about one character just as you'd meet and talk to a friend for a few minutes.

— William Faulkner

Mrs. S. and Dr. S. process into BUC arm in arm to the music of Vivaldi. She is wearing a beautiful knee-length white lace dress with a red sash. Dr. S. is in a white tux with a red shirt and matching silk handkerchief in the top pocket.

They are glowing, simply glowing, so very, very happy.

The ceremony is brief. The readings are from their favorite poets.

Mum's short-sweet sermon speaks to the beauty of two kindred spirits finally finding each other in the autumn of their lives.

"This is your time," she says in that warm, melodic voice that almost sounds like she's singing. "This is your time. Your perfect time. All that was before has led you two together. To honor and love and treasure each other. To enjoy this delightful season. Autumn. Amazing autumn." Mum pauses and seeks the face of her own beloved, Riley. He smiles and nods and she nods back.

"Of all the seasons," Mum continues, "the autumn is God's finest. The trees don their fanciest, most colorful robes and dance all night and day."

The library garden is lit by the hundreds of twinkle lights Sam helped me to string earlier. He had held the ladder so I could do most of it myself.

There are small vases of flowers from the Bramblebriar gardens and votive candles on each round table.

The food is delicious. Everyone is so pleased.

I circulate, quietly giving each guest a penny and telling them the plan.

Sam pours champagne into flutes. Ginger ale for me.

I clear my throat. "I'd like to offer a toast."

Everyone stops talking and looks to me.

"Dr. S. . . . Mrs. S., please stand here." I position them in front of the whale spoutin' fountain. The guests form an arc around them.

I feel a wave of nervousness, but then I take a deep breath and begin.

I nod toward Dr. S. "I have never heard this man say 'I love you' to this woman."

Dr. S. laughs and smiles at Mrs. S.

I nod at Mrs. S. "And I have never heard this woman say 'I love you' to this man."

Mrs. S.'s lips mouth the words silently to her groom, an action not lost on their assembled friends and family. I see my mom grab Sam's hand and he pulls her in closer to him. I look briefly at Nana, feeling how much she misses Gramp.

"But . . . whenever I am in their presence . . . I see it. *I feel it*. I know that this is love. True love. The kind of love some people wait a whole lifetime for, search the world for, wish and pray and hope beyond hope for. And you two" — I raise my champagne flute, and the guests follow me — "You have found it. Love."

I smile at them, my eyes wet with tears. I hold my glass higher. "Love. Love. Love. Love. Love . . . *Love*."

"Hear! Hear!" guests say. Glasses clink. We sip our toast.

I nod for Sam to offer the first wish. And then, one by one, each guest raises a penny, expresses her or his wish for the happy couple, and then tosses the coin into the fountain.

"Your idea?" Nana whispers in my ear.

"Yes."

"Gramp and I are so proud of you, sweetheart."

I hug Nana. "I know, Nana. I feel it. Every single day."

There's music and dancing. Lots of slow songs. I dance with Sam. I dance with Mr. S. I dance with Riley.

"Great job, girl," he says. "Great wedding."

"How's Mum doing?" I say.

"Strong as steel," he says.

"How about you?" I say.

"I'm praying," he says.

"Me, too," I say. "I just know Mum will beat this."

"Time for the cake?" my mother asks, tapping me gently on the shoulder. "It's getting late."

"Oh, gosh, yes, Mom. Thanks. I almost forgot."

"I'll go get it," my mother says. "I put it in the library kitchen."

I feel sad thinking about how Rosie didn't bake this wedding cake. How I used to put the charms in the center with the ribbons . . .

"Willa," Sam says, touching my arm. "Look."

Here comes my mother carrying the cake. A beautiful three-tiered wedding cake with ribbons streaming down.

My mother walks to me and sets the cake on the table. "I hope I did it right," she says.

"*You* made the cake?" I say.

"Oh, gosh, no," Mother says. "Our new baker, Coby Mabitu, did. Wait until you meet him, Willa. He starts tomorrow. But I put in the Bramblebriar charms just like you usually do," she says.

My eyes fill with tears again.

My mother just paid me a huge compliment.

The best wedding planner *ever* just copied one of my ideas, one of my new traditions.

I hug her. "Thank you, Mom."

She hugs me tighter. "It was a perfect wedding, Willa."

"Well, look at who my teacher was," I say.

"You're teaching me, too, honey. It goes both ways."

Sam wraps an arm around each of us. "My two best girls in the world."

When we get home, I have a message from Will. He got home safe. His grandfather's condition has stabilized. His grandmother is really grateful Will came so quickly. "I miss you, sis. Take good care of Salty. I'll be back soon. I promise."

I call Tina. She heard from Will, too. She starts crying on the phone. "I miss him so much, Willa. I think I really love him. I mean really, really love him."

"I know," I say. "I think you do, too."

"Hey, maybe we can do something together tomorrow," she says. "Oh, wait, I know. Let's go shopping. I want to see if Lammers' still has those pink sneakers."

"Sure," I say. "Sounds good."

Tina copying fashion ideas from me? Mother copying wedding ideas from me? Well, this is a most surprising summer.

Salty lobs into my room. I hug him tight. He looks at me and smiles. No, really, I'm not kidding. My dog smiles. He does.

I go get the phone and look up Ruby's number. I tell her that Tina and I want her to go shopping with us tomorrow.

"Pink sneakers?" she says.

"That's the plan," I say.

"Great," she says. "We can all match. Sounds fun."

I'm turning back up to my room when the phone rings.

"Rosie!"

"Hey, girl," she says. "How was the wedding?"

I fill her in on the details. She says she and Lilly are doing fine. Her new neighbors helped carry in all their boxes. There's a girl Lilly's age next door.

"And Lilly already started teaching her to read caterpillar," Rosie says, and we laugh.

"Tell her Aunt Willa is proud of her and I'll send her more books soon."

There's a knock on my door. "Come on in."

Sam.

"Just wanted to say what a great job you did with the wedding."

"Thanks, Dad."

"Did you write that toast yourself?" he asks.

"Yes."

"It was beautiful," he says.

"Thanks."

"You know what, Willa?"

"What?"

"You inspire me."

I smile at him.

"I've decided to start writing again."

"Really, Dad? That's great."

"Well . . . I don't know how great it will be, but I feel like writing again, and that feels good."

CHAPTER 26

Willa Plants a Garden

*Read the best books while you are young
And then, someday, when you are ready,
You will write great books of your own.*
— My Gramp Tweed

Rosie's replacement, Coby Mabitu, is in the kitchen when I report for work.

He is African, from Kenya, jet-black skin, tall and thin. He speaks so softly, I have to lean in closer to hear. There's an aura of peace about him.

"Try the muffins," he says. "Blueberry."

Oh, my gosh, can this guy cook!

After breakfast duty, Salty Dog and I head to the beach.

We run up one side of the Spit and down along the other. It's cloudy, looks like rain later. Only a few people here and there.

I lie on my towel and read the jacket copy for *Among the Hidden.*

It's about a society where it is forbidden for a family to have a third child. The main character, Luke, is one of these forbidden "shadow children" and he spends his whole life in hiding, never going out, never having a friend. Then, one day, he sees a girl's face in a window and realizes she is a shadow child, too. . . .

Ooh nice, what an interesting premise. I open the book and dive in.

"Willa."

I open my eyes. I had fallen asleep. Jess is looking down at me.

I sit up. Salty next to me, sound asleep, not much of a guard dog, that one.

"It's gonna rain," Jess says. He squats down beside me. He smells like the sun and that Abercrombie cologne he wears.

"I'm sorry I couldn't stay Sunday night," I say. "My parents wanted me home."

"No worries," he says.

He picks up the book on the sand next to me, reads the cover, smiles. "You and books."

I feel a raindrop on my face. Salty barks; he felt a drop, too. Salty's not a big fan of rain. Too much like a bath, I guess.

"Willa . . ." Jess says. "Listen. I think Luke told Joey about you and me."

You and me. "Are we a *you and me?*" I say.

Jess leans in toward me. He stares at my neck. He touches the heart-shaped locket. Before I can stop him, he opens it. He looks at the faces, me and JFK. He lets the heart drop from his hands.

"No," he says. "I guess not." He stands up.

"Jess, wait."

"Later, Willa." He walks off quickly.

"Jess, please, come on, let's talk."

He keeps on walking. I watch him leave. I want to say *stop*. I want to say *go*. Not knowing which is true, I keep silent.

The rain comes now, fast and heavy. "Come on, Salty, let's go!"

I get on my bike and we hurry home, the rain washing away the sea smell from Salty and the river of tears from my cheeks.

I shower, put on comfy sweats, snuggle under my summer comforter. Hours later when I wake up, the storm has passed and sunlight is streaming through my window. That's Cape weather for you.

I check my messages.

Joey. He says he's sorry for being mad and hanging up on me. Truth is, he sort of had a date, too, with Lorna. Just one time, nothing serious. He misses me. He can't wait to see me. He's had it with Florida. He'll be home next weekend.

Next weekend!

The next message is from Jess. He says he's sorry for being mad about the locket. He likes me, *a lot*. He hopes I'll give us a chance. He and his parents are headed out to Martha's Vineyard for a music festival next weekend. "Come with me, K?"

Next weekend? JFK's coming home next weekend.

♥ ♥ ♥

I go to my desk, get out my journal.

I write, and write, and write.

I decide to stop thinking and worrying about what will happen with Jess and JFK. There are more things to focus on in my life right now. Friends to support as they deal with cancer ... (Reason: And you were too quick to judge Ruby, Willa. She wasn't the one who told JFK. Willa: I know, I know) My brother, Will, who I hope will return to us soon ... An inn to help run ... A beautiful Cape summer to enjoy.

But what about Jess and JFK? What will I do next weekend? Welcome JFK home? Go to the Vineyard with Jess?

Let it go, Willa. You're going to drive yourself crazy.

I look over at my bed, remembering that heart-to-heart conversation with my mother. She said time takes care of everything. Just live your life and move on.

In this moment, I make a decision.

I am taking a break from romance.

I dig out my stationery and write a note to each of them saying I just want to be friends, for right now anyway. I need some time to sort things out and focus on my family and myself and that I hope they understand. I seal the envelopes and hurry down to the mailbox. Writing a letter might be a lazy way out, but, hey, I'm a writer. Writers write.

Back up in my room, I pick up my pen and open my journal again.

Mum always tells us to "get out of" ourselves, to focus on others, to think about how we can use our life to make a good difference in this world.

What can I do? I think I already decided that.

I look at my bookcase, all my beautiful books. I walk over and take down *Anne of Green Gables* by Lucy Maud Montgomery, one of my very dearest favorite old friends. I open the book, leaf through the pages. I hug Anne as if she is real. Which of course, to me, she is.

I lay the book on my desk, turn back the cover, and stick on one of my FROM THE LIBRARY OF labels. I look back through my journal for the language I got in my head that day I first got this idea, then I write:

> *Take me home, free, if you wish to read,*
> *Then, when you are finished, replant the seed.*
> *Leave me somewhere for a new friend to find.*
> *A book is a perennial thing,*
> *It blooms on and on and on.*
> From Cape Cod, With Love,
> Willa Havisham

I cut a piece of sticky label, write FREE, and stick that word on the cover.

Then Anne and I set off into town.

Minutes later I leave her on a bench on Main Street — the bench where Ruby and I sat the other night when she told me her scary news — the bench I remember Nana and Gramp Tweed sitting on when they first were falling in love — the bench JFK and I have sat on many a time enjoying an ice cream cone.

At the corner I turn around and look.

Anne is sitting there waiting.

A red bird alights on the armrest of the bench and then off again it goes.

I planted the seed,

my part is done,

who knows how this garden will grow?

Willa's Summer Skinny-Punch Pix List # 3

Among the Hidden, Margaret Peterson Haddix
The BFG, Roald Dahl
Ella Enchanted, Gail Carson Levine
Everything on a Waffle, Polly Horvath
The Fire-Eaters, David Almond
Firegirl, Tony Abbott
The Golden Book on Writing, David Lambuth
Hope Was Here, Joan Bauer
Kira-Kira, Cynthia Kadohata
Make Lemonade, Virginia Euwer Wolff
Out of the Dust, Karen Hesse

If this is a book you own, not one you need to return, perhaps you'd like to make your own Pix List of favorite books on the next page?

☺ *Coleen*

_____'s

Pix List

_____

_____

_____

_____

_____

_____

_____

_____

A Letter to My Readers

Dear Friends,

Since the publication of the first "Willa book," *The Wedding Planner's Daughter*, in 2005, and with each succeeding one — *The Cupid Chronicles, Willa by Heart, Forget Me Not,* and *Wish I Might* — thousands of you have written to say how much you love reading about Willa and her life on Cape Cod. Many of you have been inspired to visit this beautiful part of the planet on vacation; some return summer after summer, year after year; others say you are planning your very first visit to Cape Cod. I hope it is all you have dreamed of and more.

While many of the beaches, shops, restaurants, and points of interest mentioned in the Willa books are quite real places (and favorites of Willa and mine), alas you will find the town of Bramble, the Bramblebriar Inn, and Sweet Bramble Books only within the covers of the Willa books.

What you will find when you visit us are towns just as quaint and picturesque, inns just as warm and inviting, and bookstores and candy shops galore.

In celebration of the fifth anniversary of the original book, *The Wedding Planner's Daughter*, and in honor of *you*, Willa's fans and kindred spirits, I have decided to follow Willa's lead.

If you are visiting Cape Cod and perchance stop by my Cape town of Falmouth (the town I most modeled Bramble after), you may very well spot a book sitting on a bench.

If you see FREE on the cover, open it.

If there is a label inside, FROM CAPE COD, WITH LOVE, this is a gift to you from me and Willa, a seed to be planted and passed along when you are finished, and on and on the garden will bloom.

With all best wishes,

Coleen Murtagh Paratore ☺

Acknowledgments

With thanks to my brilliant editor, Jennifer Rees, who is such a *joy* to work with; to Lillie Howard for the gorgeous book covers; and to David Levithan and all of the outstanding people at Scholastic Press and Scholastic Book Clubs and Fairs.

To my wonderful agents, Tracey and Josh Adams, and to all friends of the Charlotte Mecklenburg Library, Charlotte, NC, where I happily discovered quotes about books inscribed outside the building (jotted down then and now used in this story) as I explored downtown Charlotte, NC, while participating in the wonderful Novello Festival of Reading a few years back.

To Willa's fans and kindred spirits throughout the world who write with comments, questions, and suggestions, and to ask when the "next Willa" is coming.

To my beloved godmother and aunt, Jane Spain Ducatt, who I think was the first person to introduce me to book plates and whom I am certain was the person who gave me the first book I really truly *loved*: *Little Women* by Louisa May Alcott.

To my mother, Peg Spain Murtagh, who I am quite convinced has read more books, and *loved* more books, and generously purchased and loaned and passed on more books than any one woman on the planet. Every time I visit her, she talks excitedly about at least one new book she's reading or one that I absolutely must read. Everywhere you look, there are books. Books, books, books. It's often tricky finding clear footage to the table, where we will sit for tea because there are so many stacks of books about — books she will make notes in and reread and treasure over and over again.

Thank you for sharing your great love of reading with me, Mom. You are, and always will be, my greatest inspiration.

And always, and forever, my three dear beautiful sons, Dylan, Connor, and Chris. I cherish the memories of us sitting on the couch when you were little, reading, reading, reading the books you so excitedly selected when we "shopped" at the Guilderland Public Library. Today I cherish hearing your very candid opinions about the books you are required to read in school. Keep on trusting your own inner voice. I am so proud of you.

Read on,
Write on,
Dream BIG,
C.M.P.